Two Atlanta misfits

drug dealer Boots Tu
dirty work. Phobos an ... ack,
go elbow deep in bloc ... gristle, cleaning up dog fights, delivering drugs, and disposing of dead bodies. Regardless of the haul, they shovel it, bag it up, stuff it in the trunk of their 1982 Cadillac Deville and drive it off for disposal. The misfit pair fumble their way through dangerous circumstances and criminal adventures. Desperation eventually drives them out of the city, across lost highways, encountering a circus of outlaws and revolutionaries living on the margins of morality.

Praise for Manny Torres' new novel Dead Dogs

"Dead Dogs is a fast-paced hangout novel."—***Keith Lavecchia, McNally Jackson Books***

Excerpt

One wore clown makeup with a red bulbous nose. Another wore a Viking helmet like a cartoon opera singer, and their leader was a bald, horned madhatter with a waxed mustache and a slanted gaze. He wore a monocle and held a miniature pitchfork. There was a .45 in his other hand. The others had weapons too.

Fireworks burst above them.

"I guess you're the crew," Phobos said. "Where are we going?"

One wore clown makeup with a red bulbous nose. Another wore a Viking helmet like a cartoon opera singer, and their leader was a bald, horned madhatter with a waxed mustache and a slanted gaze. He wore a monocle and held a miniature pitchfork. There was a .45 in his other hand. The others had weapons too.

Fireworks burst above them.

"I guess you're the crew," Phobos said. "Where are we going?"

"Get in. Sit down," the madhatter said, adjusting his top hat. His horns poked through the holes in the stovepipe.

Phobos obeyed. He got in, switched on the light.

The madhatter said, "My name is Pony St. Trash, the Pope of Irony. You can just call me Trash. Make yourself comfortable. It's going to be a long ride. Switch off your taxi light. Get on the highway and let's leave Clown Town to the clowns. Drive."

"Isn't there anyone else you can ride with?" Phobos said. "Kind of tired. Been driving all day."

"We're going to the coast, my good man. I was told you're the best driver to get us there." Trash feigned a weak-sounding, mock British accent. "We'll stop for coffee, and palaver with the dead along the way. We'll try not to get your car too dirty."

"Do you have to keep your guns out? I'm not driving getaway for you. If you think that's what I'm going to do you can get the fuck out of this car right now."

"Relax, curly. I'll do no such thing. We're separatists, we're nihilists, we're Stalinists. Second Amendment fetishists. We're just headed to another party on the east coast. Hang out with some friends, smoke a lot of weed, do a lot of drugs. Go on. Drive! We are on our way to start a revolution. Go baby, go!"

Chuck was still passed out when Phobos got the car moving. The country roads were dark, but he found the highway and its blurry signs.

DEAD DOGS

Manny Torres

Moonshine Cove Publishing, LLC

Abbeville, South Carolina U.S.A.
First Moonshine Cove Edition Aug 2020

ISBN: 978-1-945181-894
Library of Congress PCN: 2020913671

This book is a work of fiction. Names, characters, places and incidents are products of the author's imagination or are used fictitiously. Any resemblance to actual events, locales or persons, living or dead, is entirely coincidental.

Cover design and photograph by the author; back cover and interior design by Moonshine Cove staff

Acknowledgment

This book is dedicated to the memory of Derek Brian Lord, Atlanta artist and musician. A man of moped repairs, and many other trades. *The Trespasser.*

I'm forever indebted to Chuck Cowart and John Frevert: you are henceforth immortalized in these pages.

To Cosmic Charlie, the sweetest cat I've ever known: may you live a fuller life next time around.

This book started out as *Great White,* title by David Hood. Thanks, buddy.

Thank you to Gene D. Robinson and Moonshine Cove Publishing for believing in my novel.

Deepest love for contributions, support and encouragement:

Jesse Castaneda, Mark Castaneda, Tunica Coats, Carrie Hodge, Gabino Iglesias, Katrina Johnson, Brian Derek Lord, Aaron Marks, Amanda Goldstein Marks, Monkey, Thomas Mullen, Shanee Navarro, Puma Navarro, Diane Navarro, Khali Navarro, Penny Pine, Shauna, Carlos Torres, Albert Torres, Scharlotte Refano-Torres, Lisa Torres, and Samantha Torres.

Thank you

About the Author

Originally from Brooklyn, NY, Manny Torres resides in Atlanta, Georgia. He is also a photographer and painter. In addition to writing *Dead Dogs,* he's written articles for *My Darling Atlanta,* and written and directed several documentaries and music videos, including *The Trespasser, Unendangered Species,* and *The Abby Go Go Christmas Special.* For 15 years he was a programmer and co-conspirator on *Step Outside: The Strange and Beautiful Music* program on WMNF 88.5FM in Florida. He's worked as a photographer, sold insurance, written training manuals for a large corporation, and managed a touring rock band. He occasionally curates film and art shows around Atlanta. He is currently editing a series of crime novels, as well as a supernatural western.

https://matorresart.weebly.com/dead-dogs-novel

Author's Note

Please note that *Dead Dogs* contains some scenes that depict dog fighting. The scenes were written, not to sensationalize violence towards animals, but to make the public aware of the epidemic of animal abuse that is prevalent in the United States as well as other countries. In preparation for writing the book, I researched articles and stories in The New York Times as well as online sources. For more information concerning dog fighting or cruelty to animals, animal neglect and abuse, please contact The American Humane Society, teachheart.org, ASPCA, or the local police department.

Dead Dogs

“As I lay dying, the woman with the dog’s eyes would not close my eyes as I descended into Hades.”

Homer, *The Odyssey*

PART I: GREAT WHITE

“Nobody questions garbage juice.”

Freebird

Phobos sat like a derelict Buddha on top of the broken newspaper machine, dusty, a little greasy, a little crusty around the edges. Everything he owned was there beside him: guitar, rucksack, his disintegrating coffee cup. Chuck hadn't expected to see him back on his throne when he rounded the corner. He looked as surprised as he could, considering half his face sagged a little.

"What's up, hustler?" Chuck had a full beard now. He walked slower than he used to, hobbling with a cane. His hair was shorter, his glasses were bigger. Sometimes he stuttered.

Chuck cleared old cups and newspapers off the bench outside of the newly remodeled Bohemian Café and sat.

Phobos had his hands on his knees meditatively. Most of his face was a bushy red beard. Big eyes behind thick glasses, wool cap holding down his curls.

"What's up, dawg?" Phobos responded with a casual drawl.

Their fists dapped softly.

"It's been months, man," Chuck said. "Maybe a year? I thought you was dead."

"May as well have been. I was in North Carolina. Just got in a few days ago."

"N.C.? What the fuck is up there?"

"Family. Jail. Shit."

"Thought you was originally from Tulsa?"

"Born there. Raised in Raleigh, N.C."

"Yeah? I don't go up there much these days." Chuck

thought about it further. "Matter of fact, I don't *get out* much these days. Damn. It's good to see you, man."

"Likewise," Phobos said. "Got into too much trouble while I was up there so I came back to what I know best. What do you got going on?"

Chuck tapped his cane. His good hand touched his face. "Not much. Except a heart attack. And stroke."

"Goddamn." Phobos unfolded his legs. "That's a big bummer, man. At least you lived to tell about it."

"I guess so," Chuck said. "Can't eat steak anymore, though. Or take Molly. But funny you should show up around here. I've been looking for you."

"Hang on, man. Don't offer me anything. I'm done with drugs."

"No way, man. That's not really my thing anymore."

"It's weird hanging out here since I got back. And everybody wants to give me something or involve me in their vice. They think I'm some kind of superhuman who came back from the dead."

"I got rid of my house."

"*What?* Did you sell it? The *green* house?"

"Yeah. Same. Did you see it before I moved out? The humidity ate the walls up. It started to get moldy and shit. Neighbors came snooping around, saying they were gonna call the cops. Had to bail. They just couldn't mind their own fucking business. Can you keep a secret? Well, I guess I can tell you..." Chuck leaned in. "*I did it*. I set it on fire."

"That's fucked up."

"Had to burn it. Now, I kind of owe for the merch that got burnt up. Product. Profits. *Fuuuuck*." Chuck paused. "And things ain't what they used to be. In the trade, I mean.

I don't know anybody around here anymore. Don't recognize the faces."

"Yeah, I realized that the moment I stepped off the bus." Phobos said. "There's a new group of leeches and vultures on this fucking street, man. I tell you what. One row falls, another rises. I've been on the east side since I got back, and it's been nothing but solicitations. I just came by for coffee and random fuckers started throwing their junk at me."

"Who's trying to sell?" said Chuck. "Who's got the connect?"

"I don't know them. Last time somebody gave me free junk I almost died."

"That really sucks, dude. Hey, the free coffee at the bank is pretty good. You don't have to buy it from this 'café" if you don't want. I mean, you believe this shit? Our old place, 'under new ownership'. They got locks on the bathroom now. Prices went up. Fuck it. I get mine at the bank but I'm gonna sit *here* and drink it."

Phobos lifted his cup. "I appreciate free. I'll stand in line all day for free."

"Found a job yet?"

"Kind of." Said Phobos. "I'm back at Harold's farm. Collecting junk. Fixing shit for him. Feeding his cats and dogs."

"So, you're not working."

"I've been away, trying to resurrect myself, man."

"Glad I ran into you."

"Yeah man. Glad to see a familiar face. Changes happen. It's what it is. Not sure where I'm going next."

"I need someone to drive me around. Know any good drivers?"

"I'm just on my moped right now."

"Sweet. The old one?"

"Nah. That one got trashed. I just found an old frame, put a lawnmower motor on it and got it running."

"You're a genius man." Chuck applauded. "Anybody ever tell you that? I really just need to go to Bloomville, near Rome."

"That's a road trip, man." Phobos said. "What are you doing up there?"

"Doing some cleanup work. Maybe some low-key deliveries ..."

"No man. Nah. Who you kidding? I'm nobody's mule. Not anymore. No fucking way. Just laying low right now. Low, so very *lowoooo*... I'm laying low as fuck, man. You wouldn't believe how low. Off the map, off the grid. Harold doesn't even have power at the farm."

"I hear ya, buddy." Chuck said. "Don't blame you. What about the Great White?"

"That's my brother's Caddy."

"Hey, can you do me this solid, though? I'm sure Roy will let you drive me. And holy shit: you definitely cleaned up your game. I respect you wanting clean work. I'm proud of you, man."

"My license is expired." Phobos nodded. "But I'll give you a ride on my moped if you need it. Just don't ask me to run any illicit boxes or packages."

"Nah. It's not like that. Promise. Just come out with me to Bloomville. We're definitely going to need a car. I can't drive on account of my gimp leg. At first, I tried auto instead of stick, but then I couldn't even do that. No flex in my arm, no stomp in my leg. Plus, I lost my truck."

"Your dad's truck? That's a shame. I mean, if Roy will let me drive his *shark* maybe I can help you. Not 'til Friday though."

"All right. Can you pick me up? Around two?"

"Where you livin'?"

"My dad's old condo. Around the corner from here, and down Churchwood. It's the only thing he left me."

"Freebird's running a crew?"

"A skeleton crew. He took a management position. His uncle made him crew boss. But I'm more of an *independent* now."

They enjoyed their free bank coffee while catching up. Watched the new locals, declined handshake drugs, argued with passing crust-punks, sang some songs.

"So, you lost the house?" Phobos said.

"Yeah," Chuck said. "Bummer. Had to burn it to protect it."

"Real shame, buddy. Looks like we could both use a boost."

"Wanna get high?"

"Nah man. I told you I'm clean."

"It's just weed man."

"All right. Light it. I mean, the universe needs to cut us some slack. It's been a real bitch."

Earlier.

With or without his father, the condo had always felt empty. Rising from the easy chair that morning, cat jumping off his lap, and the sun slipping through the faulty blinds, Chuck went into the kitchen. Lots of dirty plates and empty boxes of frozen meals. His whole left side had abandoned him. Worse than the heart attack he'd had two years ago. His left leg hobbled more than usual this morning. It dragged.

He went back to the living room after moping around, but most importantly after feeding Princess. He stretched in front of the blinds: up, down, sideways, watching his new neighbors walk their dog, leaving shit where it squatted.

Back at the easy chair he put on his leg brace, looking for his shoes. Princess liked to cuddle on top of them after she ate. She was a fuzzy Wirehair with a puffy tail. When he wasn't home, she'd sit on the window sill absorbing all the sun she could. Or pretend to be a sundial on the carpet.

Putting on shoes was a struggle, and he'd left his cane hanging by the front door. When he reclined, she jumped on his lap, and they dozed. When he woke, he ate some grits and eggs. Drank some orange juice. Washed his face, scrubbed his beard, brushed his teeth. He sat back down in front of his giant TV and watched baseball highlights. Princess meowed and he rubbed her head and neck until it was time to leave. By 8:45 a.m. he got up, grabbed his cane, and decided to limp through the neighborhood.

The street was cleaner than last year. More white people moving in meant more garbage pickup and more police presence. Less gutter punks but they never really went away. They tended to blend in, sitting on the curb with their crusty baggage, broken guitars, dogs tied with rope, buckets out for change. They waved at him, he nodded back.

Years ago, he'd strutted up and down this street in ripped jeans, faded t-shirt, sporting a Mohawk, knowing everybody, talking to people who were dead now, or forgotten, or forced out by rent hikes. He felt a stranger, taking in all the new construction.

What the fuck were they opening now? $9 tacos? Who are these faces? To his new neighbors he was just an interloper. They tended not to wave, pushing past him with their expensive strollers, and dogs in tow, walking to the coffee shop or yoga studio at the end of the strip. Or tattooed, bearded white men walking fluffy dogs. Even the café had been overhauled and looked more mainstream and corporate, practically overnight.

Honey, our drug dealer lives in this neighborhood. We should totally move here. It's a great place to raise up the kids.

Teahead Tommy was still active on the strip, reduced to digging in trashcans and loitering, way past his tolerance of *tea.* Ripped pants, stained tank top, teetering sick and wobbly inside his crusty biker boots. He would tighten his arms around his shoulders so hard he'd never need a hug from anyone ever again. Old B-boy posing. In Teahead Tommy's head it was still 1986. He'd bust a move for a coin.

"Hey man, let's get dusted," he said with a clownish, curled-lip snarl that was supposed to be a smile.

"Man, fuck off!" Chuck limped past him.

Two ladies in tight yoga-wear stopped their strollers on the sidewalk in front of the bank, hindering all pedestrian traffic. A dog tied to an expensive bicycle barked at Chuck. The sudden stop made his hip hurt a little. The yoga ladies tightened their grips on their expensive handbags as he skirted around them.

The small bakery where he used to get his cookies and bagels got bought out. Must've happened while he was napping one afternoon. The girl who'd had her dad buy it for her turned it into a pet store. The gym was still there, but it'd been converted into an old-school fitness club, incorporating iron dumbbells, ropes, and balls. He could do his therapy lifts and be out in an hour. But he didn't like the looks the guys with the curled, waxed mustaches gave him.

Chuck saw a man he thought was his father, but it wasn't. The man wore a straw hat and was walking two small dogs. Chuck didn't believe in ghosts, but these days were filled with moments like that.

Chuck crossed and there was Kenny, waiting for the bank to open. He was a small black man with hyperphagia who had an incessant habit of eating out of trashcans. Most of his day was spent loitering the strip or strutting mindlessly up and down the city wearing oversized clothes from the rescue mission, carrying armfuls of discarded food.

There was complementary coffee inside the bank as part of their customer-appreciation initiative.

"What's up, Kenny?" Chuck said.

The bank manager had just unlocked the double doors. He smiled and waved them in. Kenny clapped his hands together.

"Coffee time," he said and went inside.

That long brown table inside the warehouse used to belong to Chuck. A relic from the grow house. At one end there was a spread of weapons, and on the other an open suitcase filled with spongy, purple marijuana. Surrounding the suitcase was a barrier of green bags packed with powder. Stacked next to that was a two-inch book of postage-stamps, about 12 x 12, illustrated with squiggly psychedelic designs, skulls and grotesque, smiling clowns.

"This is all we got left," Boots said, circling the table with his wheelchair. "Kinda got us fucked up right now, fam. This. Is. Everything. Had my Mexicans pull *everything* from the place they could. They even dug up the floors and shit."

"Damn, dawg. We fucked." Demetrius stood by the corner of the table, arms crossed. No laughing. Not today. The grow house had burned down, the crops were smoke.

"Yeah. Don't bring it up no more," Boots said. "I'm tired of explaining myself. Don't tell anybody, don't act like we short on supply. People want they shit, they gonna get they shit, one way or another." He pressed his face into his palm. "Bet. I always wanted to get deep in this shit, and here I am. It's not just the dog pits anymore, bruh. Now I'm forced to diversify."

"What's that?"

"What? Diversify? It mean spread out, nigga. Be open. New ideas. *Get this new bread.* That type of shit. Pay attention and you'll learn something. Imma get this. Ain't no going back now. Believe that. Survival of the fittest."

"Word. I feel you, fam."

"Look where I was and look at me *now*. Two houses, four cars, and I'm prolly gonna buy a boat. Straight up cash. I'll put a down payment on Atlanta if I want to. This loss ain't fynna break me. The merch got burnt, but I got this. This the seed to start it back up. Gonna get hooked up in other avenues. Imma use all the resources I can tap into. I ain't the only chickenhead out there serving, but Imma be the one on top. They want me to back out, knowhaimsayin'? I ain't fynna show up like no punk ass bitch."

"Yo homie, know this," Demetrius said. He'd nervously stick his hand under his arm to make sure his piece was still in its holster. "Once you with the big players, you in. Ain't no love lost if you can't keep up. They don't give a fuck."

"Nigga, *I am a big player*. Imma keep up. Fuck you think?"

"Just saying. Competition is thick, fam. You won't have your hands in things the way you have the pit, or weed."

"Nigga, I know. I wouldn't be doing this if I didn't know how to manage all this shit. You done forgot I was a lil' jit, running trains like this. It's just mix-and-mule on a bigger scale. This is where I'm s'pose to be right now."

"But dis large? Tri-city? You're fynna be rolling over some toes when distribution starts."

"Nigga, is this first grade?"

"Nah, my G." Demetrius clapped his hands in prayer. "I'm sorry."

"Imma come out like a steamroller, that's what's up." Boots raised his arms.

"True dat, bruh. You just said you ain't an amateur since you been runnin' it."

"I got all my people lined up. We even got a scientist on our team now!"

"Like Einstein and shit?"

"A fucking chemist, my nigga! Believe dat. We got a network going on. Portable pharmacy and shit. We goin' legit as fuck."

"You quittin' the dogs?"

"You crazy? That's a whole other thing, and down for life with that. *Shiiiieeet.*"

"I'm down for whatever. You got this, chief. Yo', we should go to St. Thomas and celebrate. A little vaca?"

"Let's get this business straight, then we decide where we wind up."

"Imma find me a honey or two to bring with us to the islands. Bet."

"Bet."

Roy was Phobos' twin, but they looked nothing alike. Same beard, but Roy didn't wear glasses. Nor a headband. Jeans and collared shirt mostly. Loafers with argyle socks. Presentable, ready to do the work.

They stood in between towers of packed boxes. More than a dozen cats snaked around their legs.

"Can you take those?" Roy asked. The house smelled like cat piss and mold. Roach traps and dust.

Four heavy boxes sat at Phobos' feet. Practically immovable.

"The fuck can I do with them?" Phobos said. "I got here by Greyhound." His rucksack dangled by his leg. Boots were untied. He considered tying them but didn't want to bend over. He wore a faded purple serape and had tucked cigarettes in his black headband like bullets.

"I don't give a shit," Roy said, wondering aimlessly around the mess, trying to make sense of the ephemera hoarded over decades. "Cait is gonna take the cats and look after them. But I can't do anything with these records. I don't even like Elvis."

"It's not Elvis." Phobos scratched his head. "This shit is really old. These are 78's. Old as fuck and really heavy. Mostly country, and blues shit. I mean, I don't hate it but I don't have a storage place for them."

They dragged what they could to the front porch.

"Cait's going to grab the rest and talk to the real estate people." Roy said. There had been no eye-contact since Phobos had arrived.

"Why isn't our dear sister keeping the house?" Phobos said.

"Or the cats?"

"She doesn't have to." Roy shook his head.

"Fuck her. She's not even here to help. She's always leaving us with all this shit."

"She just moved to Nashville and just got married. Go easy."

"Really? Did you go?"

"Yeah. Didn't you get the invite?"

"You think I get mail in the tent I live in? She tends to forget there's two of us. Takes flowers to her old boyfriend's grave but never sends me a birthday card."

Roy stared at him intently. He listened very intently. "You just said—"

"Were you there when Mom went?" Phobos asked. He rested against the screen door. A moth flew across his nose.

"Yeah." Roy kicked the flaking linoleum. The old wooden floor of the porch showed through. "I watched them pull out her tubes. Walked with them to the morgue afterwards. I had to have her cremated. It's all I could afford. Those graves are like buying little plots of land. She didn't leave a living will so I had to convince them that's what she wanted."

They moved underneath an awning at the side of the house. Grass was overgrown. In the middle of it was a rusted lawn mower.

"So, you're not going to take the records?" Roy said.

"I'll just pawn them." Phobos said. "Can you give me a ride down there?"

Roy drove him in his giant Great White Cadillac, dropping him and four boxes off at Value Pawn. He helped unload.

"Guess I'll see you at the next funeral," Phobos said.

Roy shrugged.

"Was no funeral." He said. "Just a few crying people standing around her deathbed."

They shook hands and Roy drove away. They didn't see each other for several months.

The shop was messy, dimly-lit. There was a stack of Watchtower magazines on the counter beside a crowded ashtray. It took the man sitting there some time before he looked up.

"You Mexican or something?" His name tag said Ron.

"No." Phobos looked down at his scuffed boots, dirty jeans, and serape. "Why?"

"That thing you're wearing. Should be wearing one of those *Chihuahua* hats with it. Hehe. Got some in the back."

"This poncho? I got it at Sears. I ain't Mexican. Nothing wrong with them, but I'm not Mexican. You think you can give me something for these records?"

Ron leaned over and gave them an indifferent look. He said, "Got any Black Sabbath or AC/DC?"

"I don't know that my mother listened to those bands."

"Those look kinda old and dusty." He leaned on the counter. "I mean, you gotta understand."

Phobos pushed back his glasses.

"So, nothing?" he said. "Can I just leave them? It's not like I can take them with me. I'm traveling by foot. Getting back to Atlanta by bus. Can you gimme a few bucks for them?"

"I don't think I'll be able to resell them, you know? It's not that I don't want to help you."

"Okay. Well, can I just leave them here?"

"Well, push them to the side and I'll dump them later."

When Phobos walked out in the late afternoon, he cut diagonally across the deserted parking lot to a gas station. An abandoned Tastee Treat kiosk stood across from it, a giant soft-serve cone that had grayed over time. He entered the gas station and bought a PBR tall boy and went back outside to drink it. Above him was a faded Greyhound bus sign and itinerary. He sat on a wobbly bench, surveying the parking lot, observing a great, abandoned America. The sun was shrinking, and his rucksack felt full of rocks. He reached into it for a book. When he shifted, the weight of the rucksack fell against the bench post and it crumbled. Slats fell. He stood up in time to see the bench collapse under a cloud of dust. The other post fell over the stack, completing the rubble sandwich.

"Hey man!" Immediately the clerk inside the station half-stepped out of the door. "You broke my bench."

"Nah man. I sat... well, I was going to sit and the thing fell and broke. And then the other thing fell and broke."

"You broke it? That's vandalism."

"Nah man. It was an accident."

"It's fucked. Look at that! Why don't you just go ahead and pay for it right now. You been drinking?"

"I was going to. Just got one sip is all. Remember? I just bought this from you? I don't have the money to pay for that. I'm homeless."

"You're loitering too. This ain't no fancy patio, *hipster*."

"I can see that." Phobos said.

"I'm gonna have to call the cops."

"Really? Come on, man. It was an accident. I swear, I don't have any money for it. I'm heading out of town on the last bus tonight. See the schedule there? That's the one

I want to be on."

The clerk went in and grabbed the phone from behind the register.

Phobos downed his tall boy, spit some of it out, and started walking toward the avenue. In a short time, a cop car rolled past him. Phobos thought he'd sprint across the avenue to the abandoned Pizza Hut but his sack was too heavy and he was full of beer bubbles.

They searched him and cuffed him and took him back to the gas station. The clerk was heated, yelling,

"Fuck this guy! He got drunk and crazy and broke my bench!"

"Excuse me..." Phobos said. "Uh. Listen. That's not how..."

The cops and the clerk stopped their conversation and turned to him.

"I really have to pee," Phobos said.

"Stay here," one cop told him.

"Well, yeah. I guess I don't have a choice. But if I don't go now, I'm going to pee here and then get a ticket for it, or pee all inside your patrol car."

The cops looked at each other. The one holding him nodded and let him back into the gas station.

"Thank you," Phobos said and was led to the back past the stacks of boxes and a filthy mop bucket. Cuffs were loosened and he went inside a water closet that hadn't been cleaned in the past 55 years. The oily sink barely trickled when he tried to wash his hands.

Phobos was escorted back to the front, uncuffed. He pushed open the front door and sprinted across the parking lot. He got thirty yards when he tripped over his unfastened shoelaces, tumbled and rolled. For that one second, he was glad he'd left his guitar in Atlanta. The heavy rucksack kept him anchored to the pavement. When he looked up the cops were standing over him. The wires of the stun gun came straight at his chest, but he didn't remember anything after that.

"Six months," Phobos said outside the café, drinking free bank coffee.

"Six months?" Chuck said. "For some piece of shit bench that you accidentally broke?"

"They found some liquid epoxy in my bag and convinced themselves it was black tar heroin. Another trumped up charge. All that time locked up was just me was waiting for bail that never came because I never had it, or anyone to give it to me. And the trial was months away."

"Did you call your brother?"

"He was already on his way back to Atlanta. He's got a kid now. No time for me."

"So, how'd you wind up back here?"

"I went to trial six months later but I skipped out on the sentencing. I bummed some change and got on a bus. One of those shitty buses that don't even have a bathroom on board."

"You're basically a fugitive then." Chuck tapped his cane.

"I guess. They don't extradite you for that kind of shit. That happened in North Carolina, not here."

"Jesus, man. Can I buy you a cup of coffee? Like a legit cup?"

"Sure, man." Phobos scratched under his cap.

"But this thing I got," Chuck offered. "Should be good money, man. Fast money."

"This isn't like with your cousin, right? I'm not shoving coke balloons up my ass, or running hustle tables or selling bootleg porn. Didn't he get shot in Virginia or something?"

"Yeah." Chuck laughed. "But he was a total shit head, fuck-up. This is different. No ass-balloons. Quick cash. I know you could use it. It's funny though. You? A fugitive? *Bahahaha!*"

"Yeah, fucking hilarious." Phobos smiled. "Whatever you got I'll probably do it. *Probably*. I gotta get used to being back on my feet. At least if I wind up dead on the strip no one would be surprised."

The sun set and they sat there making up blues songs while Phobos played guitar. Hippie-caveman Wayne Beardo greeted them. He shared his joint and danced like a fool, spinning around, telling them he'd be moving to Colorado with his nine cats.

"I don't like the shit they're passing around," Beardo said. "It's some zombie shit and I can't deal with it. Can't smoke it." He dug up a coffee cup from the trash and went inside for a free refill.

Phobos and Chuck made fun of slumming tourists and the new locals. Collected change in a paper bag Phobos had set out. Later, a trio of young girls circled them. One started singing along to their deconstructed blues, the other danced, another sat cross-legged, smoking crack on the curb. One schizophrenic hobo danced to Phobo's discordant strumming and weird rhythms. He stopped and screamed at them until Chuck bought him coffee and a muffin to calm him.

When it came time for them to depart, around 2 a.m., when things got really sketchy and criminal, Chuck went limping home. Phobos left the opposite direction on the moped he'd rigged with a lawnmower engine. Across town on an otherwise pleasant late-spring night.

No matter where he woke up there was always dirt. Harold was up before him, grumbling and shoveling and picking up scattered junk. Phobos didn't remember a time he saw him sleep. He had his own house on the other side of the farm. Sometimes there was power, sometimes there was no water. This morning Harold was moving, shuffling like a prospector. He was ancient but only in the sense that he'd enjoyed the 1960's and had taken enough LSD to reshape his DNA. Ancient in wisdom when it wasn't a speedfreak rant, like a hippie Methuselah.

Phobos had fallen asleep on the workbench, his head on his elbow, guitar at his feet. Still wearing his glasses. The sun was bright in his face through the open door, casting silhouettes of Harold, his cats and dogs, and the work bucket he carried to clean up the garbage that accumulated in the yard.

"I don't mind scraps," Harold said. "I don't mind the tools, and engine parts lying around, though I'd prefer them in the shed. It's the litter that gets on my nerves. We're isolated here. I'm trying not to be like the outside. Don't wanna be accused of being a hoarder." He wore a sagging gnome hat, overalls rolled up to his knees, and brown mud-crusted boots. He picked up litter—cigarette butts, soda cans, etc.—with a claw attached to the end of a stick. He used an ancient handkerchief to wipe his neck and brow. "Good morning, by the way. Can you get the coffee going? I see you were burning the midnight lamp."

Phobos stood, stretched, and accidentally kicked his guitar. He grunted, picked it up and put it on the chair. Then he turned on the hotplate, leaned into the orange coil and lit a cigarette.

The coffee kettle was probably older than Harold.

"Hey, how long has this coffee pot been around?" Phobos said.

Harold looked up from his cleanup.

"Before me," Harold said. "Been around since my granny. Maybe it belonged to her mom. They came from Uruguay. Brought it with them. Or maybe bought it here. I remember drinking coffee from it as a kid. Before school. Yep. Caffeinated since school days."

Phobos took out the black sock from inside the pot and turned it inside out, dumping the grounds. He shook out the remains and refilled it with fresh coffee from a tin. Poured water from the standing water cooler and then got the ancient pot boiling.

Soon they sat on paint buckets, smoking and sipping. Harold brought out his guitar and they played some spontaneous blues. He had a way of rapping out words that meant nothing. Random observations, a list of the things he saw in the yard, people he missed. Songs about his old dogs and cats, and the possum that crept around at night. Phobos shared some bagels he'd dug out of the trash at the coffee shop. He toasted them on the hotplate and they smeared peanut butter on them.

After that, Harold ran errands in his dusty old van and Phobos finished repairs on a lawnmower and hedge trimmer. Then he worked on a tractor that sat on cinderblocks. Once he got the engine going it worked the water pump. He then installed a makeshift sprinkler system for the garden and a shower inside a small shack built from saltine cracker tins and wooden crates.

Harold returned with a box of dented cans he'd collected on his run. They sat and played music again.

"They think they're civilizing us, but we civilized ourselves," Harold sang. "We been holding down the east side longer than anybody else out there. Before you or Chuck, there was Cosmic Charlie and Chinacat, and Beardo. We're the only ones left."

"The progress grows like leprosy, man." Phobos said. "You seen all those yoga studios? There's one on every block. Bums get kicked out, yoga studios go in."

"They could've just extended the park or built a clamshell for poetry readings." Harold said. "Some folks trying to tap into something holy with all those yoga shops. The holiest."

"*Assholiest.* No joke. There's a bakery down there that sells $8 cupcakes. I usually dig mine out of a dumpster, so fuck them."

"Even the pushers gonna get pushed out." Harold put down his guitar and walked over to the tractor engine. He admired his reflection on an oil slick by his feet. "Haha. Look it my crazy face. Where have I been?"

Phobos laughed. He helped Harold clean up the rest of the yard, sweep the pavement, and then spread out tools for the needed repairs. Worked until the afternoon. Cleaned up afterwards. Rested on the paint bucket, smoked cigarettes, played guitar, petted cats.

Harold washed up under the yard hose. Drank water from it. His home was a chrome Airstream in the back of the yard. He went in, put on a fresh shirt, pants and a different hat. A checkered bowtie. He grabbed his guitar and said, "Let's hit those tourists with some tunes. Like they ain't never heard."

They strutted to the village court where the out-of-towners were coming through to see the freaks on parade.

Chuck met up with Phobos frequently over the next two weeks.

Another morning, another round of coffee going lukewarm while they vacillated. Kenny huddled with them, giggling. He ate a donut he'd fished out of the trash.

"What was up with that dude yelling like that?" Chuck said. "I mean, I gave him coffee and a muffin. Kenny doesn't even get that crazy."

Kenny giggled and agreed, wiping donut glaze from his cheek.

"I don't know, man." Phobos said. "No matter how you pave this street, it's always full of lousy bums. But soon, they'll be clearing our asses out of here. We'll be paved over by strollers, sealed up in hipster mustache wax. Scoop us all up in garbage trucks like in that movie *Soylent Green.*"

"You really think that'll happen to us?" Chuck said. "I kind of think this coffee place needs us here, man. They need the street cred. It'll keep the money pouring in as long as the yuppies know they get a freakshow with their latte."

"Agreed," said Phobos.

"Yeah, but that guy was fucking nuts. Kind of scares me being out here at night."

"Hey, he's the last of his kind. Like you and me, and Harold, Beardo, and Kenny."

Chuck agreed with a prideful glow.

"But what brings a person to *that* kind of place?" he said. "You know, in their head."

"Can't say. I'm a bum." Phobos said. "But I ain't crazy.

Everybody starts out normal. But then shit just goes crazy. Everybody was a babbling idiot-child at some point in their life until things began to break. You go from sitting on the floor drooling on a bottle to sitting on a curb drooling on a crack pipe. From a stinky crib to a stinky bum."

Chuck agreed. Under his dense uneven beard, he looked boyish and callow. Like a teenage caveman. He brought a hand to his chest like he was giving the pledge of allegiance. He caught his breath, leaning on his cane.

"You alive?" Phobos said.

"Eh. It varies from day to day."

Phobos finished his coffee, saved the cup inside the large pocket of his gray cargo shorts. Chuck gave the rest of his to Kenny and patted him on the back.

"Thanks, Mr. Larson," Kenny said.

"What'd he call you?" Phobos said.

"He doesn't remember names so he calls me anything that comes to his head. He thinks you're *Mr. Carl.*"

The pair walked around the block. Phobos walked at Chuck's pace.

"I'm glad to see you came out of the gutter, buddy." Chuck said. "You're better than all that mess. I guess you and Roy are on good terms since he's lending it to you."

They came upon a gleaming white car, parked behind the café.

"Yeppers," Phobos said. "I suppose we are. As long as I don't fuck it up. 1982 Cadillac Deville. Four-door."

"Jesus. What a fucking *shark.*" Chuck patted the soft dash once they were comfortably seated inside. "Too bad the top don't come off. Comfy as fuck. So great. *Great White,* man. If it was mine? That's what I'd embroider on the side of the doors."

"You mean lettering? Like pinstriping?"

"Yeah, like Dr. Johnson used to have. You remember that old player?"

"That's corny, man. I wouldn't want anybody to think I'm a pimp or something. Try not to mess this up too much. Don't eat in here or sleep in it. Don't put your feet on the dashboard."

"We can go places with this, man." Chuck smiled. "Kind of beats your old moped."

"Yeah. But I miss that thing. I think she gets jealous when I drive this shark."

"I like what you did with that old scooter though, with that milk crate you strapped on the back. Cargo tough. Yeeeah."

"What happened to your pickup truck?"

"My dad's pickup? I wrecked it awhile back. Right before the house burned. You were out of town when it happened. Didn't lose my license at least. Didn't really report it. Truck is probably still there, wrapped around that tree. I should build a shrine around it. Like leave flowers, and fruit and shit. This car must suck up a lot of gas."

"Roy pays for it. I don't have to refuel it unless I'm outside the perimeter."

"That's a great deal, man. How's the farm going?"

"Not doing too much. Fixing up whatever broken shit Harold has around."

"That's the life. Always wanted the farm life. Me, and my cat. And *my girl...*"

"The lots overgrown, and there's a bunch of dead tractors. But it's enclosed enough. Isolated from all this shit."

"At least you got sanctuary to write your songs."

"I feel blessed and privileged. What else you got going on, Chuck? You're always on that fucking bench with me. Thought you was working."

"Odd jobs," Chuck said. "Here and there. I'm also trying to get work on movie sets."

"Pornos?"

"Nah. Legit shit. Real Hollywood shit. Marijuana Mike got a small part in something recently. Said he'd let me know."

"He can't be relied on for shit, dude. I've never seen that motherfucker sober."

"He's all right. I let him stay a week when I had the house. Sold him my dad's gun."

"Think I might get a job with that too? I like movies."

"I can ask. I'm in debt like you don't know... Remember Boots from back in the day?"

"Boots Tumbler? The rapper? Yeah. He punched me in the face at one of his shows."

"If I remember correctly, you were talking shit, man."

"He fucking sucks." Phobos said.

"You're lucky he didn't shoot you." Chuck grinned.

"Are his legs still missing? Fuck him."

"Yeah, he had that accident. They haven't grown back."

"Smoking crack while sitting on train tracks will do that."

"That's not what happened. And he hit you because you kinda acted like a dick at his show. You brought it on yourself."

"I don't remember that. I can't believe you work for him."

"Yup. When I'm not working with Freebird. Who do you

think turned my house into a *farm*? Boots has some work for me, but it's not mule work. I promise. He's got Mexicans working for him now, doing the real shit jobs."

"Guns? Girls?" Phobos said. "Is it bootleg tapes? Is he making you sell his CDs on the train?"

"Nah. He said to go see him at his warehouse."

"Is it a fight club? I'm not letting anybody beat my ass for cash again."

"Come on man, you're a fighter."

"Hell no! What are you trying to get me into?"

"Ha. Just kidding. He said it's cleanup work. Things get messy around him. No biggie. We're in, we're out. A week, maybe two. If we're lucky."

The construction of condos on the south side near the elevated train line was taking a long time to complete. Future tenants had the choice of looking at the abandoned station or the warehouses covered in graffiti. These newly constructed, giant sheds would eventually become yuppie dives of wine and fine cheese, yoga studios, artisanal coffee, bread and soup shops. In the meantime, most of the area looked like post-war London or South Bronx in the 80s. Someone had spray painted *Die yuppie scum* across a brick wall where an old building had crumbled. It was the first thing train passengers saw from the overpass.

The Great White came out of the tunnel, turned the corner and parked. The lot was an acre of bare concrete and potholes. The old warehouse had once been a train depot. There were cars parked around back. Occasionally dogs barked. One of the walls had neon pink graffiti that read *You aint shit Rico* and *Rich Nigga Dre.*

"They *are* making pornos here, dude," Phobos said.

Chuck laughed. "Nah, man. But yeah, probably."

The smell.

"Man." Phobos made sure the car was locked. He scanned the deserted back alley and together they walked to the warehouse. Phobos kept looking over his shoulder.

"I hate the way dogs smell," Chuck said.

"Makes you say that?"

"Don't you smell that?"

"This whole place smells like shit. Always has. I used to buy scag out here and sleep in that tunnel."

"Not shit." Chuck gave the place an approving look. "But right *here*. Smells like dogs. Dogs smell like...*raw chicken*. You should know, gutter punk."

"Ain't no gutter punk." Phobos said. "Or train kid. I'm just a little homeless. I hate gutter punks. They're just trust-fund kids that stop bathing for a year, and suddenly turn into enlightened bums. A group of them beat the shit out of me once and took my bike."

"Sorry, man. Shit, I didn't know you then, but I saw your bloody picture in the paper."

"I got help after that. Cleaned up, got a job, found a place to stay. The beating was kind of a blessing, really."

"Man, that fucking smell." Chuck covered his face and nose. "I guess it doesn't bother you."

"I can relate to dogs. Smelly bastards."

Chains rattled and the door rolled open as they approached the cavernous warehouse.

"Smells like a slaughterhouse," Phobos said. "Used to work in one."

Chuck looked inside and knocked on the metal frame.

"Hello? Hey, Boots?" He said. "Where ya at, homie?"

Phobos looked deep into the abyss of the loading area. He could make out two figures coming and one rolling. To their left was the shadow of the man who'd opened the warehouse door.

Moments later a large black man missing his legs below the knees rolled into the light. One eye was weak and closed, the other bright and opened. He wore an Atlanta Falcons cap to the side. There were two hulking men to either side of him, Bobo and Link. They wore expensive sweat suits and sneakers, and reeked of weed.

"What up, my man?" Chuck and Boots traded hand slaps, grips, and secret handshakes. "'Member my boy, Phobos?"

Boots gave him a slanted glance.

"I remember." Boots' voice was hoarse, but cut down to 3/4 his body size, and in a wheelchair, Phobos had to step back cautiously. "Of course, I remember dis dumb ass cracker. I beat his ass and he called the cops on me."

"Oh shit," Chuck laughed uncomfortably. "Oh. Uh. My bad. He's the one got you locked up?"

"Nah." Boots said. "Well, yeah. For one night. Then I sued him. Case is still litigating. You owe me money, muthafucka."

"Wait..." Phobos said. *"What?"*

"Yeah, muthafucka. I was doing my act at The Glaze and you heckled me. We tossed it up outback. Muthafucka called the cops."

"Yeah," Phobos said. "That is true, man. Sorry. I'd been smoking rocks that night."

"Boots, bro, *I didn't know...*" Chuck said.

"Fuck all that." Boots eyeballed them. "You muthafuckas came to do some work? 'Cause it's payback time."

"Yeah," Chuck said.

"Maybe." Phobos said. "What's the work?"

"Well, you working *off* what you owe me," Boots said. "This muthafucka Chuck ain't tell you yet? Now you can work off what you owe me too. How 'bout that?" Boots rolled backwards into the warehouse, spun around and said,

"Follow me."

Bobo and Link let them go first. Down a red lit hall that

smelled like an intestine. To a basement where silhouettes passed them by. A line of them. Leaving. Heading toward sunlight. Phobos and Chuck walked tightly side by side.

"I'm sorry, man. I wasn't...I...I didn't know." Chuck said.

"You said to trust you," Phobos said.

"Don't worry. I know these guys. Most of them, at least. They're cool."

"What's it gonna matter anyway? We're fucked."

Dogs barked. Howled. Roared. Some whimpered. Some slept. Phobos and Chuck entered the sublevel walking across moist concrete down to a circle of men. Somebody worked a hose with a heavy-duty spray nozzle. Another man worked a wide broom over the red concrete. Dog cages lined either side of the arena and the barking had grown deafening. Boots parked and his bodyguards stood close. It got dark a few seconds, damn near pitch-black when the lights blinked.

"Got your rabies shot, my guy?" Boots said.

The concrete was permanently stained. The space stunk of rust, open sewage, rancid cologne, bleach, and dogs. The smell of primal men, the scent of beasts. The howl of dogs echoed through the corridors. Two Mexicans wearing jeans and leather vests swept and hosed the floor in tandem.

"Always get your rabies shot," Boots said. "A man gets tired of reaching out to a rabid bitch just to get his hand bit when he's trying to be nice."

"Jesus, Boots..." Chuck turned green, on the brink of leaning over and hurling. Just to the side of the pit was a raw and bloody stack that needed removal.

"It was a busy weekend." Boots said.

"Um, do we get an apron?" Phobos said. "Or gloves?"

"Come on, fool," Boots told him. "Just grab some trash bags and go for it."

"My leg..." Chuck was ignored.

"But what about the Mexicans?" Phobos said. "I don't wanna take their jobs."

"You won't, because you're not getting paid," said Boots.

"What are *they* gonna do?"

"Fuck does it matter to you? They gonna make me tacos or some shit. You don't have to worry about them right now, muthafucka."

Phobos lit a cigarette and got started. Footnote to his resume'. Worked as a cook, dishwasher, crime-scene cleaner, flyer distributor, sign-holder, barback, bouncer, pizza man, janitor, DJ, street busker, panhandler, gutter punk, train kid but—

"I've never cleaned up after a dog fight."

All free labor. But it would keep him alive. Work was work. Phobos embraced it. Lit another cigarette and kept working. Chuck did the same, slowly, meticulously. Sometimes one-handed when his left side failed him. The Mexicans stood back and watched, laughing while Chuck did the hosing. Phobos carried trash bags full of carnage to the parking lot and shoved them into the trunk of the Great White.

"Should have brought my rain boots," Chuck said working under low lighting, sloshing through gooey blood tea.

"La proxima ves, pendejo," one of the Mexicans said.

"Every time I see you or we hang out," Chuck said. "We wind up around dead things."

A week later. Warehouse.

Phobos held a shovel in his sweaty, bloody hands, scooping remains into a garbage bag Chuck was holding.

"You're the one that brought me here, man." Phobos said.

"I said I was sorry, but this is always how we always wind up. Dead girlfriend, dead cousin, that time you OD'd on heroin..."

"I didn't know what it was," Phobos said. "At least I didn't die. Or maybe I did. Because this is obviously hell."

"But the other two guys died."

"I got lucky..."

"'Cause you're fucking *immortal*, man." Chuck raised his arms in praise and almost fell over. "You've gotten first, second, third chances. You ever know other people like that?"

"Dead people?"

"No, lucky people who don't die."

"My brother is luckier than I am."

"What about me? People who have people die around them all the time? A lot of people have died. Around me."

"Well," Phobos said. "People die all the time."

"I mean, like people around *me*. I've watched other people die many times. I've been around a lot of dead bodies is what I'm saying."

"Sure. It's been a busy death year around me too. So, we

going to keep dropping these in dumpsters?"

"For now," Chuck said. "Dumping in someone else's dumpster is illegal."

"Dude, dog fighting is fucking illegal. What the fuck are we doing with ourselves?"

"We're not fighting them, dude. We're cleaning up. Somebody has to do it. But we can't keep going back to the same dumpsters every time. They'll find the *leftovers* and trace them back to us."

"Who's *they*?" Phobos said.

"I don't know. People who find bodies. Kids. Dumpster divers. That's why Boots is moving from this location. Up west. More country area. Less heat over there. I talked to Freebird about finding us new locations. He's been working with different brokers, and body counts are rising. It could be a good, busy summer for all of us. If you want to make some cash you can keep, we can probably help him dispose of *his trash* as a tradeoff. Cross-partnership to bring peace among the groups. It's win-win."

"What kind of trash?"

"Don't ask."

"Fuck." Phobos wiped his forehead with the back of his hand. "Who are these groups you're talking about?"

"The Council for Local Narcotics Entrepreneurs. Or whatever they call themselves."

There were voices just outside the rolling metal door.

They'd finished filling eight garbage bags when Chuck said,

"Think this'll all fit in the Great White? When me and Freebird used to cruise around we'd make drop-offs all over the place. Just find random dumpsters. You know, same science we apply now. Only one time did anybody ever find a body part. A foot. Sometimes we had to *chop-chop* to fit the body in a bag. Me and him did a lot of disposal work before I worked for Boots."

"I really don't want to scuff up my brother's car."

"We won't. These are soft bags."

"It's starting to stink, though."

"Well, we can pick up a shit load of scented tree fresheners at a dollar store. I like vanilla myself."

Chuck picked up one last dog. Brindle-coated from what he could make out under the blood.

"What a waste of an animal." He said.

Another dog barked outside. Then the half dozen caged ones barked back.

Outside, they could hear Boots talking.

"These bags are fucking heavy," Chuck said carrying one at a time through the entryway. Phobos carried two in each hand. There were several corridors branching out from the center of the warehouse where the pit was. Once upon a time the tunnels had led to loading depots for trucks and trains. The giant service elevators frequently jammed up and went down to a hell they'd yet to experience. The cavernous spaces smelled strongly of blood and garbage. Chuck often liked to play *"what's that smell?"* with Phobos as they walked down these dark corridors. Could be garbage, shit, sweat, spit, dried or fresh blood.

The high metal door had that greasy diesel smell to it. Phobos yanked the chain and slowly pulled it open. On the concrete landing outside Boots and his two bodyguards were talking with new arrivals, a slim black guy with glasses and his Dominican girlfriend.

"We cool?" Chuck said trying to hold up his bag.

Boots nodded at them when they passed thru.

"We need to talk," he told them. "Later."

Phobos held his head down but looked at the massive Pitbull that the new arrival held on a chain. The thin black guy had on plaid short pants, designer tank top and black flipflops with white socks. He anchored himself, struggling with the chain wrapped around his arm. The dog was velvety gray with a white collar.

"Lando, the fuck Imma do with ten PlayStations?" Boots said to the guy holding the dog. He kept eyeing the Dominican girl with her short jeans and black curls. There was a detailed tattoo of a black panther wrapped in the Dominican flag on one of her thighs.

"If anybody can move them, you can." Lando said.

"The fuck you get all that? You been lifting shit from Walmart again?"

"Haaaa...no. *Tell him...*"

The girl stepped up, with the menace of a bantamweight boxer. All big shoulders, rocking her head back and forth, giant loop earrings jingling.

"I got a man working deliveries with DHL," she said. She emphasized each sentence by punching her open palm. "All he gotta do is pretend to lose a box, and *bam*, PlayStations all day and night, son. Discounted for you, Boots. Buy in bulk."

Boots stroked his fuzzy chin. The nod came slow and pained.

"Nah." He directed himself only to Lando. "I'm straight, my guy. I've evolved myself these days. I ain't got time to be pushing petty theft. I'm diversifying my business. And just so you know, we ain't competing here no more."

"Where you moving the fights to?" Lando said.

"I'll let you know in time, my nigga. And what did I tell you about showing up unannounced? Imma throw your ass in the pit if you do this shit again."

"Dawg, I need a stack. We drove all the way in from Jonesboro."

Boots chuckled. "Fuck I look like? Do it look like I give a fuck how far you drove, nigga?"

"Dis dog my moneymaker right here. You know how many bricks I had to sell to buy him and raise him?"

"One? What happened to your job at Walmart?"

"Fuck that. I got fired."

"You was working the sporting section. That's a no-brainer, nigga. How'd you get fired?"

Lando fidgeted. The frantic dog kept yanking him.

"See, what had happened was she got the job there after me," Lando said. "And then come to find out they had warrants for her but since they needed help for Christmas, they didn't bother with a background check. So, they kept her until New Years, you know what I'm saying? Then, later they discovered her outstanding warrants and escorted her out in cuffs. She on probation now."

"What were the warrants for, shorty?" Boots said.

"I beat a bitch ass in Oakland City," she said.

"So, how'd you lose *your* job?" Boots said to Lando.

"A nigga's always guilty by association."

"For the time being, maybe you should piggyback on her SNAP card. Or trick her ass out. Do something. Simple facts. Ain't no more fights here after today, bruh. It's getting too hot up in this bitch. Plus, too many cracker-ass crackers coming out to see these fights now. You know how that shit goes, more crackers, more trouble. White people love ruining shit for niggas."

Lando dipped back, placed his hand on his chin, still holding the dog by its impossibly thick chain.

"Yo, let me axe you dis," Lando said. "Can you give me an advance?"

"Advance?" Boots twisted his head dramatically at his bodyguards. "Muthafucka, is you ill? How Imma pay you for a dog that's probably gonna lose?"

"Nigga naw. This a certified champ."

"Certified?"

Boots and his men laughed. "By who? *Yo mama?"*

By then Phobos and Chuck were at the Great White.

"Seriously, bruh." Lando said.

"For real," the girl said.

The dog tightened harder on the chain. Lando pulled back and then... released. The dog launched into Boots' neck but caught his forearm instead. Bodyguards were too slow responding. The girl jumped at Bobo, Timberland boots landing square on his chest. He fell back five feet and then she tore into his throat with her manicured talons, bits of gold splintering everywhere.

Boots pulled out a piece from his side and shot Lando, killing him instantly. He pressed his arm and then shot the dog. The bullet tore through the animal's center and exited into the head of Link's head and then through the eye socket of the Dominican girl who'd wrapped herself around him. She froze in midair with a strange twisted look on her face. Boots let her have the rest of the clip and she fell against the concrete like a pile of bloody rags. He reloaded and then shot Lando again. Blasting both dead bodies several times until he was satisfied. Then Demetrius came out shooting from the warehouse. Bullets sparked and bounced off the walls filling the entryway with a din of echoes, and more barking.

"Nigga, you useless!" Boots yelled while reloading. He circled and yelled, then shot at the sky. The dogs inside howled and barked. "Get them two clowns back here! Tell 'em to make space in their trunk for these four niggas."

"How 'bout them PlayStations though?" Demetrius said.

"Yeah. Get that shit out they car. Give them shits out as door prizes for the next round of fights. And then take the car out to the Bridge to Nowhere and drive it off the edge."

"How 'bout you get them crackers to do it?"

"Nigga, how about you do what I say?"

"We send messages back and forth all the time. But we're not together-together." Chuck said.

"Wait, is this the girl from China or her sister?"

"Nah, I got a new one that's really special. We're in love, but she may not know it yet. I'm still waiting on the official word that I have been dumped by the other girl. She's from Laos, not China by the way. I still have a box of my shit I need to pick up from her place. If the bitch hasn't thrown it out already."

"Just break it off and start fresh," Phobos said. "*You* make the move. That's one worry I don't have. No attachments, man. Be free."

"Now that I think about it, it's better that I lost the house. That Laotian chick was throwing parties every night, boozing it up. This other girl, this *woman*, I met her when I had my stroke. She was the nurse who helped me. Gave me a bath, brought me breakfast. She was really nice. Black girl with funky neon hair. For that one moment I felt like a goddamn king."

"You felt royal when you had the stroke?"

"No, when I was in her caring hands."

"Sounds nice," Phobos said. "But shit, you're in worse shape than me."

"But I ain't no bum, man."

"I didn't call you a bum. You just gotta take it easy."

"Yeah, I know." Chuck said. "It was the grow house, and the girl from Laos. All that crazy shit. I was being unhealthy. No more fat steaks and no more purple Colt 45 for me. Hey, there it is." He pointed.

The Great White circled the roundabout at the back of the apartment complex. The dumpster was locked and there was a garden of trash around it.

Phobos said,

"You sure it's okay?"

"Sure, man," Chuck said. "Me and Freebird always brought shit here. Nobody cares. The girl from Laos still lives here. In fact, I lived with her for a while, 'til she changed her mind and found some other clown. That's her place over there. I should go take a shit on her doormat."

"Pay me ten bucks and I'll do it."

"I'm kidding, man. That's rude."

"You still have the key for the dumpster?"

"No. Just use a crowbar."

"I don't know if there's one in the trunk."

"There's one dangling from a chain next to the dumpster. They don't give a shit here. They'll fix it next week and it'll be broken again, like the front gate was. Look at this shit. Why do people have to live like this? You think they give a shit if we throw away a few dead bodies?"

"I don't know about this one, man." Phobos turned the car off. He looked behind him, scanned the parking lot. It was barren.

"Easy, boo," said Chuck. "This here is one of the many secret spots me and Freebird used. We're good. Trust me."

"That's what you told me before you got me this job."

"Be brave, brother."

Phobos broke the lock with the crowbar. They carried trash bags and two rolled up carpets over the concrete ramp leading to the giant green dumpster. Then two more carpets. Long, heavy trips, Chuck working with only one hand. He tossed the small trash bags in first. The carpets fell on top of the garbage with a thud. One of them bounced off and rolled down the ramp. Phobos cursed and went back for it. Chuck stared into the abstract shapes and colors of the compacted trash. There was a blue arm squeezed and fossilized among the bags and boxes.

Phobos carried the carpet over his shoulder.

"That's not one of ours," Chuck said, pointing at the arm.

"There's no fucking room here, man."

"It's been a busy season. I'll call Freebird."

"We're going to run out of dumpsters."

"Don't worry, man. It's a big city. Freebird said he was scouting out some new places."

Freebird arrived an hour later, driven by Flames in his purple Z28. Chuck and Freebird talked it over and Phobos carried the carpet to the car. After some bungy cords and a few prayers, the carpet stayed fastened poking out from the trunk. Freebird saluted and they drove off.

Back in the Great White, driving to East Atlanta, Phobos said,

"I'm satisfied just doing nothing. Living on nothing. Being nothing. Being no one." He was sour with sweat and garbage.

"But you don't do *nothing*," Chuck said. "You fix tractors and write music, man. You sing. You clean up. You're in the disposal business. You're in the 'human recycling business.'"

"Yeah, whatever, I'm just a bum. I look and smell like one. I didn't *aim* to be this way. I just defaulted to it. Life is good? Life is neutral. Life sucks. Life fucks. It fucks you."

"It does." Chuck scratched his beard. "It is and I'm satisfied with honest-to-good work. Money. Bitches."

"I don't like to talk about money. It's filthy and evil."

"But you need it. And I have another business proposition for you."

"Aw, man. Come on."

The sun went down, and the sky turned a dark blue. They listened to low country songs on the radio. The DJ had good taste. Townes Van Zandt. The Flying Burrito Brothers. After a little crackle the radio played "Pride of Cucamonga" by The Grateful Dead.

Traffic lights glowed inside the car.

"You say that a lot," Chuck said. "You say you don't know, but you know. You're here now, doing it. And we'll do it again tomorrow."

"This is slave labor, man."

"Well, we'll get out of this and then we'll start bringing in money some other way. Start doing more work for Freebird. He always pays on time."

"I guess. I really don't really need much."

"You're a minimalist, man. I know."

"I get by." Phobos shrugged.

"We'll pay back Boots and then we'll be done with him. No need to have two or three gigs at the same time. One solid, good job and then boom. We can vacation in Mexico. *Mexico,* you hear?"

"Is he still in the hospital?"

"No, but I've been avoiding him, to be honest. I told him we'd see him soon."

Phobos sighed. "Sure. Mexico? Why not Costa Rica?"

"Too many white people in Costa Rica," said Chuck.

"You ever been to Mexico?"

"Hell yeah. Carnival cruises to their beautiful beaches.

Nice looking ladies down there. Soon, brother, soon. Can't forget Boots, though. He's got a lot of fight left in him."

"Him or the dogs?" Phobos said.

"Well, he's not talking much on account of a dog ripping him apart. But hey, a train took his legs a few years back and he made it out alive. He's all right."

"You're unable to say anything bad about anyone. Sometimes, you have to pass judgment, Chuck."

"Sure, man. Wanna grab a bite? I feel like some fried chicken."

"You motherfuckers are doin' a'ight," Boots said, comfortable in his mobile chair, bandaged and gauzed, arm in a sling, neck in a brace. His voice was low and gruff. Demetrius was off in some corner texting.

Phobos stood arms crossed, twitchy like a tired schoolboy. He was wearing all black again. Shorts, tank-top, headband; faded tattoos he'd scratched himself with a makeshift needle of his own design.

Chuck's face split with a slow, massive grin.

"Thank you, boss," he said.

"Taking on more responsibilities. I like that." Boots threw them a handful of loose cash. "That's gas money. But you still owe me."

"Whatchoo got for us now, fam?" Chuck clapped and rubbed his hands together.

"Slow your roll," Boots said. Demetrius chuckled from the corner. "Bet. You know who Koi Pond is, right?"

"Like the fish?" Phobos said.

"Nah, bruh," Boots said. He sucked his gold teeth.

"We know Koi." Chuck said. "I worked for him. He had a greenhouse on the coast. He's my boy. I used to hang out at his house all the time. BBQ, movie nights, fart parties. He's got a pool. But he's all the way out in West River."

"Right. Good." Boots sucked his teeth. "Go see him. Talk to him again. Butter him up. Also, take this to him."

Demetrius threw a small box at them. Chuck caught it. Phobos looked worried. His eyes looked giant behind his bifocals. He started nibbling on his warped thumbnail.

"What's that look, man?" Boots said to him. "You can't take a gift to a friend? He's having a birthday and I can't make it."

"It's not that..." Phobos said.

"Well, I'm not in your feelings right now, bruh. But you'll take it to him anyway."

"It's cool, man." Chuck said, patting Phobos on the back.

"Whatever, man." Phobos said.

"We got you, boss," Chuck said, slowly backing away, back towards the Great White.

It took almost a full day for them to drive out to Koi Pond.

Later, by a Redneck Riviera.

"I'm sure this isn't my first time here," Phobos said. "But I don't remember the last time I was here."

"I remember," Chuck said scratching his beard. "Cops got called. Lost my shirt, my shoes, my weed."

Cars crowded the gravel lawn; beer cans, and barbecue smells. Inside were whirling lights and bubbling lava lamps. Koi Pond, the Filipino with a goatee and mustache, wearing a pink velour robe, greeted them. A stereo made in 1977 blasted the soundtrack record to *Heavy Metal* at full volume.

Koi hugged Chuck and looked at Phobos.

"Didn't think you'd ever show your face around here." Koi told Phobos. He stretched his neck out, jokingly closing in on him. "What's the matter? You don't like Don Felder? Come on. He was in The Eagles. You don't like this music?"

"It's all right," Phobos said, looking around. Two fat chicks in bathing suits ran around a table crowded with food, wine, and giant marijuana buds. There was a two-foot nug sculpture made up to look like cactus. A man who looked like Jesus walked around with only a shirt on.

"Is that Freebird?" Phobos said. He looked at Chuck and then at Koi. Chuck nodded not sure why he'd just stared at his dangling weight for that long.

A young Asian kid walked around eating Doritos out of the bag. A few minutes later he was dancing with an upside-down blowup doll with a beer can sticking out of its prosthetic vagina.

People poured in from other rooms to dance and get stoned. A blonde hippie dude named Doodah Man sat on the arm of a chair, wearing fringy cutoff shorts and a tie-dye, waving his arms around as he spoke. Koi had crowned him Doodah, The Hippie Prince. Two or three people sat around him, clinging to his every word as he presented a dubious history of rock and roll.

"The Who drummer, *Kenneth* Moon was in Led Zeppelin before he joined Jimi Hendrix," Doodah Man said.

"You don't say?" some chick wearing a Native American feather headpiece said. Her dropped jaw quivered, following along with his every word he spoke, like lip-syncing to a bouncing ball on TV.

"There is no known footage capturing how quick he was," Doodah said. "Like Bruce Lee, he could not be photographed."

"What about those movies he made?" Phobos said grazing around the group. "They slowed the camera down to capture him."

"But when he was with Led Zeppelin..."

"Bruce Lee was in Led Zeppelin?"

"But when *Kenneth* Moon was in Led Zeppelin and they played Woodstock they had the technology to capture it."

Phobos made a pinched face and then went back to what Chuck and Koi were talking about.

"What do you boys have for me?" Koi said.

Chuck handed over the cube, smiling. Koi struggled but popped it open. There was a chalky ball not unlike a bath bomb. There was a smile and two X's for eyes carved on it.

"Ah shit. Hell yes!" Koi pogoed and spun. "You guys want a snort? Man, what a nice guy that Boots. Remembered my birthday and all. Fuck if he's going to move in on anything of mine, but this was awful nice of him." He held the bath bomb and scraped some off with his nail and snorted.

"Happy birthday, man." Chuck said. He looked at Phobos and they both agreed to stay. They melted into an uncomfortable plastic-covered sofa and inhaled from a vaporizer. They grabbed snacks from bowls at either side of the sofa. Rice crackers. Wasabi peas. Doritos. Popcorn. Chuck wound up drinking a whole bottle of wine and flirted with Koi's skinny blonde girlfriend while Koi was at the other side of the room making out with the Asian kid.

Phobos and Chuck watched stragglers come in and out of the house, all wearing bikinis or nothing at all. People moved like sped-up film as the pair inhaled repeatedly from the vaporizer. They eventually shared a plate of seafood with a giant fish head staring at them. Phobos dug out the eyeballs and crunched on them contently.

"You met Jake yet?" Koi said, dancing next to them. He stopped and stood over them smoking from glass blown into the shape of a dragon. The tip of his nose was pink with Adderral. "He's that guy I told you about. Remember, Chuck? You remember. You snorted some shit with him at my Christmas party."

Chuck blew out a puff of smoke and gave the nozzle to Phobos. Chuck said,

"He jumped the fence and crossed all eight lanes of I85 and lived to tell about it."

"Yeah, haha," Koi said. "That's him. The night of the Iron Maiden show at Lenox Arena."

"What?" Phobos said as if he'd just woken up. It was more of a *whhhuuuttt?*

"Come on outside," Koi said. "He's on the patio just bullshitting. You know how crazy his stories are. Everybody's out there now. The Professor should be stopping by later. Maybe. Jake's great, though. One of the craziest storytellers I know. Fucking hilarious. Yeah, you gotta see this guy. Some crazy shit."

They floated to the backyard through the sliding glass doors.

"He was a roadie for Molly Hatchet," Koi said. "Crazy stories like he hung out and smoked crack with Bobby Brown. Man, the things he says! Just outta control. Bahaha."

Koi left them there without introductions. More people came and went. Some jumped the fence to get in. Doodah kept going into the bathroom to rinse off his legs and arms because he'd convinced himself that every hippie chick that touched him was rubbing a dose deep into his skin.

"The Professor's shit is potent..."

Bobby DJ showed up wearing a flipped-up cap, a wetsuit and flippers. He procured some compact discs and began to play music behind two CD turntables.

"Wanna go swimming?" Chuck asked Phobos.

Side by side Chuck and Phobos shook and shimmered like waves of heat and melting rainbows.

"I don't know." Phobos said. "Did you realize the pool has no water in it?"

"Huh. I saw waves. Waves. And... Jesus without pants."

Koi swung around again.

"Hey," he said. "Wanna go down to the beach?"

"Beach?" Phobos said. "You mean the Redneck Riviera?"

"No. The rich people beach. It's not too far a walk. There's phosphorescent plankton out tonight. Trust me. *Hilarious.*"

"I don't trust the beach sometimes," Chuck whispered to Phobos.

"How come? It's gorgeous."

"It is. Maybe it's the water. My father was inside the belly of a whale once."

"Get the fuck out—"

"I'm serious dude. He used to go crabbing in the Atlantic and one day he swam out too far. For a moment he was swallowed by a whale... then it spit him back out. Bitter old dude."

A stream of laughter and giggling seemed to roll over the crowd outside. They sat around the edge of the pool talking, smoking, drinking. Freebird was skateboarding inside the dry pool, a pantless Jesus with his long fuck-all beard. He dipped, came up and stood at the rim of the pool, holding his skateboard. Stood there like a swinging Captain Organ. The steady drone of conversation soon turned into him talking about cats.

"...they're our betters, man. Believe it." He said.

In the listening circle was Jake, Koi, a few women beautifully stoned, and a bald man looking at his phone. Koi's topless girlfriend had fake breasts that protruded like tan volley balls. Chuck was convinced she was a robot.

"Animals are adapting," Freebird said. He lectured while his tackle swayed rhythmically. "We've dedicated ourselves to fucking up their environment so much so that they've had to evolve *despite* us."

"Dogs and cats living together," Koi said and slapped Jake's back. *"Amirite?"*

Freebird impatiently paused. "But seriously," he said. "I've seen birds make friends with dogs. Goats with rabbits.

Cats riding horses and goats. It's fucking insane and we need to listen. Pay attention to that. *It means something!* I mean, what the fuck? We blew it, so may as well leave it all for them. The animal kingdom is saying that we can't do shit to help them or reverse environmental damage, and we certainly don't know how to be nice to each other. So, they're teaming up and helping themselves. We ain't gonna do it. We fucked everything up. Am *I* right?"

Lots of stoned nods and murmurs before he faded out. Somewhere inside Doodah Man said, *"We're all just riding through the semen of life, man. Morrison said that..."*

Chuck's eyes were heavy. Phobos was lost in the movie playing out before him.

Jake turned out to be the most taciturn and subdued of all them. Maybe it was not his night. Maybe he'd run out of material. Bored, *boring*, quietly looking like he was going to fall asleep.

"Hey, whatever happened to James?" Koi said. Everyone looked up and he unleashed his shaved testicles much to their disapproval. He laughed the hardest. They groaned and threw beer cans at him.

Chuck said,

"Gay James? In the screamo band?"

"Yeah." Koi said, tucking back in.

"He's in a cult now, I think. Long, fuck-all beard. Singing in some death metal band. He owes me money."

"He owes *me* money," Freebird said resting his bare ass on his skateboard at the edge of the pool.

"He owes *everybody*," Koi said. "Everybody owes everybody. Checks and balances, Freebird, *amirite*?" Standing up, he said, "Hey, let's all go down to the beach!"

They paraded down a gravelly street, a mile from the shore, stoned jesters, naked and half-naked, swinging hula hoops, pogo sticks, glow sticks.

The phosphorescent plankton was neon green. Glowing, shimmering off their wet skins. They were there until dawn. By then everyone had lost their clothes. Giggling until sunrise.

"I feel like I've been here for weeks." Phobos said on the beach one morning.

"We've been here since Friday," Chuck said.

"Really? Fuck. Aren't we due back for a cleanup?"

"Probably. Feels like everybody I ever got high with in high school was here."

The sunrise formed orange lips on the silver clouds. Soon it would eat the morning.

"Kind of sick of this shit," Phobos said.

"The beach?" Chuck said. "Fuck's wrong with you?"

"Nah. The house. The party. Koi's an asshole. I'm sick of him always flashing his balls at people. That shit was old when we were in high school."

Chuck laughed. "That's how it goes, man. That's just him. Ignore it. Fuck, Freebird is always losing his pants."

"Yeah, but it's expected. I think Koi instigates him."

"Of course he does. He pushes everybody."

"Anyway, I gotta take the car back to Roy. Freebird wants to ride back with us."

"We'll probably have the usual haul waiting for us," said Chuck. "There's always shit to clean up. I just don't want to go back to Atlanta right now. It's nice here."

"At least it's not North Carolina. I'm running out of places to go. Gets risky every time I go somewhere else."

"Well, shit, I run the risk of falling on my fucking face every day, but I get up. You don't see me quitting, do you?"

"Boots knows what he can get out of us, Chuck. And Freebird does too."

"Yeah, I know. What's he going to ask us to do next? I don't know. And that's the risk, brother. If I owe, I owe. You owe. Gotta stay with it until it's paid off. And I have a long way to go."

"I'm cutting loose after all this," Phobos said. "Crossing the border."

Next week, more or less.

His shoes had a rubber sole so he wouldn't slip on the lab floor, but it wasn't exactly partywear. He switched his goggles for regular eyewear. The convention was tomorrow anyway.

Mobile homes, often made from vinyl and gypsum wall panels, have a way of decomposing and *sinking* slowly into the soil where they sit. The smell of a disintegrating mobile home, particularly ones sitting on marshy soil under a tree, is something fungal that can't be named. It is more of a *flavor*.

The Professor had seen messy dorm rooms and flooded basements and laboratories before. He was glad to have those rubber soles on today. Nothing had prepared him for three feet of stacked dirty dishes and garbage, nor holes on the floor, nor the small closet brimming waist-deep with soiled diapers. Beer-can towers, newspaper mountains, and a hump of spent vials for diabetic treatments stolen from a pharmacy. Handprints and blood streaks covered the walls. Water-logged ceiling panels sagged or were missing, exposing wires covered in spider webs, and rat droppings. Flies all green and buzzing.

The sun was obscured by newspapers glued to the windows. The ceiling fan squeaked like bicycling mice. The fan lamp rattled but lit the living room. The dim bulb in the open refrigerator lit the rest.

"I was going to install another kitchen in that back room 'cause it's roomier back there." Taylor rested against the blackened stove. His tank top was neat and clean even if he wore greasy pants that hung off his ass. He had neck tattoos that slithered and snaked around his ears and face. Sleeves of stick-and-pokes covered his arms like Paleolithic art. His ten-year old son, Tyler, dressed the same, even had Bazooka Joe tats from his shoulders to his wrists. Tyler sat on a milk crate chewing bubblegum, cleaning and loading a .38 revolver. The clicking and rotating of the cylinder was nervous and frequent, but it weren't no toy, and the look on his Kool Aid-stained face was deadlocked and cock-serious.

"Mr. Taylor, I know you came a long way to show me this place, but I don't think it's going to work out for me." The Professor's face pinched with disapproval.

Taylor had the same look on his face, pinched like some yellow-toothed rat.

"I mean," The Professor said. "It'll make a good lab, no doubt. But the *location*"

"Thought you said you was hiding from some people." Taylor said.

"I am. For now. Until the trend passes. I'm looking to do some experiments and a quiet place to hideaway for a while. You got anything solid concrete, back in some swamp, hidden away?"

"Not really, chief. This is the best offer I got right now." Taylor spit tobacco juice into the opened refrigerator.

"Sorry to have troubled you." The Professor cleaned off a pile of broken boxes and a dozen palmetto bugs scattered.

Tyler, the son, kept clicking, cleaning. Reloading. Pink bubblegum glitching in his mouth.

The Professor opened his case, shuffling through his collection of stamps.

"Who's all after you?" Taylor asked. "I might could have some of my boys help you out."

"My guess is probably several former students upset at their grade from last semester. They can't dispute it because, well, I've gone missing and don't plan on going back. I think I'll be okay. I don't want to involve more parties in this matter. It's a dog-eat-possum world nowadays and I wouldn't want to trouble you. Here, you can have a sheet. It's potent. Sell it or use it."

"Shit yeah."

A gun went off and The Professor ducked.

"Tyler, what the fuck?!" Taylor looked over at the living room.

"Sorry, dad." Tyler said without looking up. "I'm trying to tighten this pin."

"Is it safe?" The Professor said.

"Sorry, sir. Kids. You know how it is."

The Professor nodded. "Now I know why there are beer bottles propped up outside by the mailbox."

"Gotta start them out young. You wanna trip here?" Taylor said.

"It's a start," The Professor said. "You can test this stuff out. It's pretty new. Potent." He gave him half a sheet and then let one dissolve on his tongue. "How about your kid? Does he want to try?"

Tyler looked up and the gun went off again. The Professor winced. It felt like heartburn. Then he fell sideways onto a pile of garbage.

The father and son team dragged The Professor outside. They put him inside his old yellow Datsun B-210 and pushed it out and away from the trailer and parked it by a dumpster.

Hours later The Professor woke up from the pain at his side, bleeding. Taylor and son had vanished. He revved the car in a panic and stomped the gas pedal, almost driving into some woods. He put it in reverse and skidded out of the lot. He ran red lights realizing he was late for the convention, and then smashed into a phone pole.

"It's fine. It's fine. Everything is fine, I'm free. I'm free."

PART II: IF DOGS RUN FREE

“I’m more interested in not bleeding to death”

The Professor

Gibton had one video store. Where Hilsboro crossed Lysson St. there was a gas station. A group of Mexicans had set up a barbecue taco grill on the back of their truck. Day laborers would stop and eat and drink from colorful bottles of Jarritos. The L-shaped plaza on the other side of the street was where the vacuum repair shop was. Gorilla mannequins stood at either side of the opened door, faded over time to a sickly green fur. Across from there, at a 45-degree angle inside the video store, Danielle leaned over on the counter flipping through a fashion magazine. She hadn't paid attention to the door jingle. By the time she looked up The Professor had walked up to the counter and plopped down his briefcase. He immediately pushed a bloody business card at her.

She'd been humming a Green Day song when she saw it but wasn't surprised.

"It's fine. It's fine. I'm free"

"Sir, you're bleeding on my counter," she said.

"Just water," The Professor whispered. "Water, please."

"You can get some at the gas station over there. All I have is 7UP." She pulled back a little.

His gray suit was blood-stained. He had brown curly hair and purple prescription sunglasses. One nod and he slid across the counter and fell like timber.

When he came to, he found he'd plugged his thumb into a bullet wound below his rib cage. He was in a car she was driving, sipping soda from a cup. It could have been later that day or ten minutes later. He'd stopped keeping time. His briefcase lay on his lap.

"I'm going to get you help." Danielle said, driving.

"What? Ha! No, not today. I can't go to no doctor. I'm lying low, dying low. Turn around now. I don't even know what town I'm in. Not from around here, you see."

"Don't worry. I know someone. If she's not busy, she'll see you. No questions asked. But we'll have to travel pretty far to get there."

"Do you always have bullet-riddled men ask you for clandestine medical care?"

"It's kind of a given, in Gibton. You'd be surprised. A lot of people shoot themselves in the foot and all. Second Amendment advocates and such."

"Who's minding the store when you're not there?"

"That's what the 'out to lunch' sign is for."

"But we just met. Where are you taking me?"

"Drink your soda."

After that long weekend on the Redneck Riviera, probably Tuesday or Wednesday. Phobos parked the Great White in front of a basketball court in Atlanta.

"Thanks for the ride." Freebird was wearing loose shorts and a black shirt with the sleeves cut off, carrying his basketball. He dunked a few, working up a sweat while Phobos and Chuck watched from the car. Phobos chewed his thumbnail wondering what was next.

"Almost done." Freebird said. He cursed and growled every time he took a shot and missed. He yelled at the ball like he was breaking up with a girl.

When Freebird's free throws came to a sweaty conclusion, Chuck and he walked and talked. Phobos stayed in the car.

"Good shooting, man." Chuck said.

"Sorry that I was yelling, buddy," Freebird said. "I've been stressed out with this new promotion. Hard to keep track of who the fuck is doing what, and what the fuck is going where. Barely have time for me."

"No worries, boss. You paid your dues. We've had some wild rides. Cleaned some fucking messes. *You're* the boss now. You got this."

"You're damn right we've seen some crazy shit. Gives me a rush thinking about it. But I hate all the driving and the stench of dumpsters. Glad I moved up from that. Putting my kids through karate school right now. Had to shut down my DJ business and I don't cut grass anymore. Essentially, no side hustles. Just management. And then, who knows? Maybe I'll start wearing suits and ties next."

"Big-baller, shot-caller. Hey, listen." Chuck stopped.

Freebird had known him long enough to recognize what his tone meant, and what he wanted.

"You did us a real solid," Chuck said. "I wanna personally thank you. But, uh, that carpet we handed over. Where'd you dispose of it?"

"You know I don't reveal sources," Freebird said. "Makes for too much accountability. But we're family. You should always know that I'm here for you. Truth be told, with all the dumpster shortages we're having, it became obvious that we needed to outsource. It's hella un-American, and I hate to do it, but time and space is money."

"You sent them shits to India?"

"Ha. If I could. Those people get enough of our garbage already. I saw a documentary just the other night about all the American garbage dumped in the Middle East. Iran or some place in BFE. They were *paid* to keep our garbage in the Middle East, you understand. Paid to take our precious American trash. They figured the desert was the ultimate solution. I would swear to you that the kid they interviewed about dumpster-scavenging was wearing a Quiet Riot t-shirt that used to belong to me. I recognized the ketchup stains."

"Sounds fascinating," Chuck said. "Did you dump the carpet in a river?"

"Polluting's not my thing. I caught Flames doing that and canceled his ass. He's got no fucking clue, the slob. I've sent a few loads to Bardo. Had to drive it myself. You know, Clown Town?"

"The Carnie town?"

"Same. Some big shit went down in Florida and we had a truckload to haul. Dumped it in Bardo. But that's another story. I don't have reliable people right now and can't be doing all the driving. Crossing state lines with a load like that is risky. But what are we gonna do?"

"So, you want us to do the transporting?"

"We'll talk about it soon. If he wasn't family, I'd roll Flames up in a carpet too. You should consider going into management, Chuck. You've been at this long enough. Pays more, you get more free time, travel pay, executive decision-making. I'll talk to my uncle about it."

"Well, I'm between companies now." Chuck said. "Boots has me locked in for a long time until I pay him off. But I need to eat. My cat needs to eat. Hard to be available to you like I want to be."

"Ah, the old conflict of interest. I can't speak on behalf of my uncle and how he's handling the competition with Boots. That legless bastard. My hands are tied on this, buddy. Otherwise I'd love to bail you out. You're welcome to stay part-time with us."

"Yeah. No problem. Either way it's a living."

"Exactly."

"So, you'll just be hauling them out of state?"

"Let's just say there's storage in Bardo that we can use. For what we got coming, buddy, we need a fucking landfill."

That morning the sun was perfectly aligned, the clouds faded. Phobos was up early helping Harold fix a tractor. He scrapped a lawnmower and used the parts for various projects. Afterward, he and Chuck sat inside the Great White which was parked on the property. Between them was a pile of ketchup, mustard and relish packets. Chuck had just put away two hot dogs.

"Doctor said I shouldn't, but I love those things," he said.

Phobos agreed. After several silent minutes he said,

"Harold is a nice guy." He peeled the corner of a relish packet and squeezed the contents into his mouth. Then they took turns sucking on various other packets.

"He is," Chuck said. His teeth were yellow with mustard.

"He let me stay here when I was recovering." Phobos sucked on a spicy ketchup pack and squinted. "Did you get those from the Crisp Dog on Hill Street?"

"Yeah. Next time I might go to the Long John Silver's next door. Their cocktail sauce is boss."

"Yep."

"I talked to Boots. Called him."

"He's still breathing? How much do we still owe him?"

"Dude. He asked if we wanted smuggling work. Like, smuggling people. The living and breathing kind. He said it'd clear the debt super-fast."

"No man. Trafficking? Fuck that. Uh uh. Smuggled people wind up dying in the trunk of your car. Fuck that. This trunk is already haunted enough as it is."

"Relax. He was feeling us out," Chuck said. "Trying to get a reaction about it. I told him probably not."

"You told him right. Shit. Did he threaten you? He can barely move around now. What's he going to do? Sick Demetrius on us? Didn't Boots catch rabies from that dog attack?"

"How could I tell? He's always fucking pissed."

"He wants to see how far he can push us, Chuck. What we'd be willing to do out of desperation. He's been starving us on purpose. We'll always be just contractors to him, man. *We're not black.* He's not going to bring us on board like his other boys."

"Doesn't mean I'm going to disobey him. He's nuts man, I don't have to tell you. Don't sleep on him. He's got goons. I've met them all. Big black goons. He said before he did any of this that he used to take mercenaries out on tours of South Asia. For a fee he would drive them in a jeep and let them use his machine gun and find some random village to shoot up. Let some of those guys relive Vietnam War memories."

"Wait." Phobos said. "I told you that story. From my friend Thomas. It's all bullshit. Like when you told me your dad shot down the Hindenburg."

"Dude. My dad never lied to me."

"Have you been smoking again?"

Chuck looked at him. "Oh. I forgot to tell you. This is completely off subject, but Marijuana Mike needs a ride."

"I'm not a fucking cab, dude."

"There's $30 in it."

"Are you fucking kidding? Thirty dollars?"

They were silent during the drive. Marijuana Mike lived with several roommates who sat around smoking from a totem pole bong, playing video games all day. He came downstairs wearing a black suit, Rude Boy fedora, and sunglasses.

"Hey," Chuck said. "Looking sharp, bro. Where to?"

Mike was already lit and smelled of booze. There were spaghetti sauce stains at the front of his suit jacket and crooked tie. He mumbled, *"Trailer park in Lakewood."*

"Is this a pickup?" Phobos said.

"Nah, man. Fuck outta here. I'm an actor. This is a movie set we're going to."

Mike sat in the back and they drove. Chuck rubbed his thumb and finger at him. Mike handed him some crumbled paper money.

"How's it been?" Chuck said.

"Been filming this shit for three years," Mike said.

"Goddamn."

"Last scene is being shot today."

The location was much farther out than Phobos had expected. Chuck danced around his aggravation. Told jokes to try and cheer him up. When they finally made it to the trailer park in Lakewood a small crew was set up. Lights, camera, people in ball caps carrying equipment and tape, a small Asian guy carrying a long microphone.

"This a porno?" Chuck said.

"Fuck you, man." Mike popped some pills and left the car.

"You wanna watch them finish?" Chuck said.

Phobos shrugged. He parked and they were allowed to watch the filming. Marijuana Mike started to fluctuate. He popped more Xanax when he thought no one was watching. He plopped on a couch and drooled his lines. His character was supposed to be dying and it was worse acting than a third grade Christmas pageant. The grips and director fed him his lines. After they wrapped, Mike tried eating at the craft table and kept drooling chips and salsa on his boots. He drank a beer and threw it up all over his suit.

Phobos watched him come undone. In turn the cast and crew watched them with contempt, wondering when they were going to drag Mike back to the suburbs. They drove back late that night, the car reeking of vomit.

Rome was getting a makeover. New condos loomed where the old train depot had been. The corner store had gotten a new whitewash coating. The faded cigarette adverts had been replaced with posters for a locally produced kombucha company. The front door had a digital ding instead of the old bell which had dangled over the entrance for decades. Nola left her gray pit bull terrier, Agee, tied outside.

The store smelled like vaping oil and incense. She gave the owners her quaint but silent wave. They knew her as the snake lady, patron saint of all the beasts, war-veteran, the portable caduceus, Lua of lost and wounded creatures. Sometimes they mistook the snake around her arm for jewelry but either way kept respectfully distant. Weren't too many black people around here, certainly not witchy black women who kept a menagerie of mammals and reptiles. If neighbors had a cat or dog injury, they knew who to take them to.

Nola put canned food and toilet paper in her basket. She picked up groceries, inspected them, placed them back. Prices had increased. New items that they'd never sold before. Curious items, snake oil for yuppies.

A cement truck drove past the store. Then another, followed by a dump truck and a van filled with work crews. Agee barked at them.

"They ever gonna finish rebuilding?" Nola said placing her goods on the counter, mentally calculating the increases.

"Seems like the construction is never-ending." The lady behind the counter said. Her husband shook his head and went into his office.

"Who can afford them?" Nola said.

"New businesses moving into Rome. That's who them new homes are for. They'll have a cattle-call soon enough and you'll see a parade of new neighbors flowing in. People moving in from everywhere. We've had two offers this week. I know eventually I'm going to have to accept one of them."

Nola paid $20 more than she usually did for just the basics.

"See you next week," the lady said.

"Goodbye," Nola said. "Cats needed their food. Agee is quite a monster to feed."

Walking back home with him she passed a sign she hadn't seen earlier, offering new homes starting in the low $400's.

Discarded bricks and construction debris littered the sidewalk all the way to her property. At the edge of the road she rolled her ankle on a brick, falling sideways, scraping her knee. One of the passing cement trucks honked at her. She took a deep breath and cursed. Agee whined at her face while she dusted off. She grabbed the groceries and limped back home. She locked the gate behind her and went inside. She cleaned her knee and went outside to feed the yard animals. Agee ran around the acreage while Nola tended some seedlings.

She sat on her back porch drinking water. Agee approached her and she whispered to him, rubbing behind his ears and hindquarters. He smiled and panted. He licked her wound and laid at her feet like a good boy.

"You ever get tired of just hanging out all the time?" Phobos said. He drove the Great White through midday traffic.

"What the fuck else is there?" Chuck said.

"You said you're seeing a girl. Go visit your girl."

"She's not really my girl. She's a woman I have a crush on. And she lives in Rome."

"Italy?"

"Georgia."

"Is this like a school crush? How old are you?"

"Fuck you, man. You sound like my grandmother."

"If she's your girl, go visit her. Bring her flowers. That's what women like, right?"

"She's not like that."

"They're all like that."

"Trying to get rid of me, man?" Chuck said. "You don't want to hang? Thought we were partners. I ever tell you about that time when I was in 7th grade and Terry Tucker invited me to a sleepover but didn't let me come to his birthday party the next day? That's what it feels like when you don't want to hang out."

"Terry the Killer?"

"Yeah. He's doing twenty-five-to-life in Fulton now."

"Did he kill anybody at the sleepover?"

"Nah. He killed some guy in a fight he picked."

"He invited you to a sleepover but not his birthday party?"

"Pretty much. Probably just wanted to watch me sleep. He still sends me Valentine's Day cards from prison. True story."

They made it back to the café on the East Side that afternoon, and from their hobo thrones watched people until they got bored. Tired of the same coffee, the yoga pants, the strollers and poodles. Kenny wasn't around. Harold was hiding in his depression cave. Wayne Beardo must have finally moved to Colorado like he said he would.

"Fuck it, let's get out of here." Phobos drove them back to the farm, which was just a few minutes away. He cooked minute rice over the hotplate. He hovered over it, tasted it, then set it aside. When it was done, he opened a can of beef ravioli in tomato sauce and poured it into a small dented pot and cooked it until it bubbled. They sat outside on milk crates eating from plastic bowls. They watched five or six cats roaming around and playing among the car parts, gutted tractors, and mopeds; car batteries, garden tools, piles of wood and cinderblocks. Projects Phobos would eventually get to.

"You should wire up those mopeds so we can ride off together, like in *Easy Rider*." Chuck said. He gulped down some sweet tea from a can.

"We won't make it out of the city in those things."

The sun throbbed at the 3 o'clock position. It was warm and humid. They were playing a round of hobo chess using nuts, bolts and pieces of broken bottles on a checkerboard when Freebird walked in like Jesus through the gate.

"Don't get up," he said. "I'll show myself in."

"What's up?" Phobos said.

"Yeah," Chuck said to Phobos. "I told him we were here. You don't mind, right?"

“Nah. I don’t care as long as he’s not selling *shit* on the premises. He’s wearing pants. That’s a plus.”

Freebird came at them casually. He wore aviator sunglasses and a sweat suit jacket with the sleeves cut off. He’d trimmed his beard and long hair. He looked like a young, hippie Steinbeck.

“Gentlemen,” he bumped fists with them. “You guys don’t look too busy.”

“Eh,” Phobos said. “Passing the time like a pile of tires.”

“I hear you.” Freebird said. “Say, how’s the car?”

“Parked over there. Keys in the ignition.”

“Yeah, because that’s safe...”

“Ain’t no one gonna fuck with this place, man,” Chuck said. “It’s protected by gnomes and faeries.”

“I see two of them right here. Haha.” Freebird said. “Still. You gonna use it today? You driving anywhere?”

“We got the day off.” Phobos said.

“How about you run me somewhere? I’ll give you gas money and I’ll buy you lunch at Subway.”

“We just ate. Where you headed to?” Phobos said.

“I'm taking you boys on a trip. I want to show you something. Some *place.* Amazing business opportunities. I’m making an executive decision here with this expansion. Changing a few things around. No one will know about it except us.”

“I got nothing going on.” Chuck said looking at Phobos. He stood up, stretched, and limped over to toss his empty bowl into the recycling barrel.

“Let’s go,” Freebird said. “The map is in my head.”

Phobos looked up at him, eyes pinched.

“You wanna drive?” he said.

"Nah. You drive. It's not my car anymore. How's she running?"

"I think the AC might need fixing. But it goes. And it goes good."

"Okay."

"Okay."

Phobos cleaned up some of the scraps that were lying around. Freebird and Chuck walked outside the gate where a big black Lincoln Continental sat idling. Flames sat behind the wheel blasting the radio, singing along to Bon Jovi.

"Whoa, is this the executive limo?" Chuck said.

"Flames totaled his Z," Freebird said. "This is my dad's. Help me with this." He opened the trunk. "Remember our first cleanup?"

"Yeah." Chuck said.

"That was the day we separated the men from the boys."

"You chopped that guy up so he'd fit in the trunk. I got sick and barfed."

"The garbage bags were too small, so we used a tarp."

"At least I got to keep his boots."

"Look at this." Freebird grabbed a can of disinfectant spray and fumigated the trunk.

"Here? In broad daylight?"

"Daylight keeps the vampires away. Let's get him into the Caddy. You guys don't mind, do you? I couldn't find a carpet, so I laid him in a blanket. I know you're busy working for Boots and all."

"Not at all, brother." Chuck said.

"This is some weird shit. Just look at him"

"Huh." Chuck looked inside the trunk. "Where's his face? Was he playing with rats after he died? Goddamn. I've never seen anything like this."

"We're taking him with us."

"Who was he? Is that Gay James?"

The dead man wore a brown suit with a green satin tie. His shoes were gone, and he had on fancy socks. He had thick hair and long beard. Whatever had eaten his face had eaten around everything but his beard. His fingertips were chewed off. He looked like a Halloween porch decoration.

"That's not for me to know, Chuck." Freebird said.

Freebird wound up driving the Great White anyway. Phobos sat on the passenger side and Chuck angled forward from the back, balancing the conversation between them.

"She's driving good," Freebird said. "You been keeping her greased. Good job."

"I keep her greased, on account of all the goddamn driving I do," Phobos said.

"We must be ninety miles out of Atlanta," Chuck said. "Where are we going?"

"Well," Freebird said. He frequently looked in the rearview like he was being pursued. "I wanted to take you guys to a place a little out of the way, where I sometimes party and where some of our trade happens. It's all fun and chuckles now, but this is a business trip."

Chuck looked at Phobos. He put a finger gun to his temple and shook his head. Phobos shrugged.

After driving most of the day they came upon a sign that said **Bardo: Welcome to Clown Town**.

"For real?" Phobos said.

"Yeah, dude," Chuck said. "For real."

Central Avenue was a capillary of biker bars, tarot shops, and craft stores. A close-knit row of made-over roadside motels covered with movie-studio facades. Hand painted designations over open doors, like **JAIL**, **GENERAL STORE**, **BARBER**, **SALOON**. The town had been built next to an old train that ran alongside the strip like a mechanical vein. Rows of parked motorcycles. A pink Sherman tank with a silver Christmas tree stuck in its turret. Trucks with animal cages in the back. A flatbed trailer with giant speakers on them. There was a shuttered church and an open lot where someone was washing an elephant. Clowns and jugglers, illustrated men. Local folk art and the tattooed eccentrics who sold it. A PT Barnum panorama right out of a postcard.

"Look at these freaks." Chuck said. "They must be preparing for county fair season."

Freebird gave him a look. "Don't judge, peg-leg. These are legit working folks. We're here by invitation. There's some personal items we have to transport out of Bardo."

"We?" Phobos said.

"Move it where?" said Chuck.

"Hauling it off and away." Freebird said. "I'll tell you all about it after we meet up with the mayor."

"We better not be taking guns or drugs across state lines," Phobos said.

"Nothing of the sort," Freebird said. "We just have an abundance of leftovers to relocate."

"Population fifteen-hundred," Freebird said. "The Honorable St. Bardo runs all of it. He's got his hands in everything. He runs a lot of business in and out of here, and he's certainly been a loyal partner to my uncle. I'm just looking to grow further with him."

Christmas trees lit up, season-appropriate, along the strip. An impromptu parade came marching out of the bars down the main street. Freebird parked at the dead end of the street where the locomotive had jumped off the tracks and settled. They walked slowly back up the midway, absorbing the sights, sounds, smells, and tastes of the scintillating arcade. Chuck enjoyed a corndog and then an *elote.* Phobos smoked a cigarette. Freebird flexed and winked at pretty girls.

"Y'all boys heading to St. Bardo's place later?" A girl in a lame' bathing suit handed them Jell-O shots from a bandolier belt strapped across her shoulder.

"Of course," Freebird said, smiling. He took his shot and the one Phobos refused. Chuck took his shot but it accidentally went over his shoulder onto the ground.

"It's his birthday, and we're doing a titty contest later." The girl said.

"Nice," said Freebird. "Wet t-shirt?"

"Nah. Just titties out."

By the time they made it to the last bar at the end of the strip they were in a courtyard arena where a group of musicians played songs by Hank Williams, Waylon Jennings, Loretta Lynn, and Elvis. A tiny woman in a red sequins dress and cowboy boots sang her heart out.

They drank beer by the buckets except Phobos who drank all the root beer there was. They cheered the titty contest and then wound up at St. Bardo's table. He wore glitter chaps over a turquoise and black western Nudie suit. His silver teeth gleamed, and his hair looked like plastic gold. St. Bardo's bodyguard, Vegas, stood by the bandstand in a blue satin shirt, blow-dried blonde quaff sitting like a crown. Billy daKid, all 4'9", bent over the pool table sinking every one of the balls consecutively. He wore skin-tight Wranglers, haircut like Moe Stooge, Skoal can circle in his back pocket. His twin brother, Bobby daKid, stood by, losing money each round. A disagreement erupted with someone at the bar. Bobby twisted his pool cue and it turned into a small sword. After a mild tussle at the bar several people were removed and the party continued.

After shots, they walked to St. Bardo's office at his invitation. It was inside one of the train cars, with shag carpet and wood paneling. Low-lit and crimson like a steakhouse in Los Angeles in the 1960s. St. Bardo sat behind his desk. It was hard to tell where he was from. He'd adapted a southern accent but maybe he was from South Africa or Chicago. His twang was comforting though at times his glare was minatory.

"It's nice of you fellows to pay me a visit on such a festive evening," St. Bardo said. "But what I've been trying to tell ya is that I can't host you anymore. I'm sorry you drove all this way to hear that."

Phobos and Chuck stood behind Freebird. Chuck'd had too many shots and was teetering back and forth, anchored by his cane. Phobos was dry, trying to absorb the antiquity of the office.

“I’m turning the storage facility into a supermarket and organic grocer,” St. Bardo said. “Nothing personal to your business, but your boss will understand. I’m at capacity as it is. Not storing anything for anyone. I can’t. There’s just no zoning for it.”

“I knew this was coming,” Freebird said. “How do you suppose I can transport the cargo? And where?”

“Well, I figured the least I could do is have you see my friend in Falfurrias. As far as transport goes, I'm going to loan you one of my vehicles.”

Freebird looked back at his crew and then back at St. Bardo. “Where, pray tell, is Fall Furries?”

“*Falfurrias*, Texas. *Tejas*, as the natives call it.”

“That’s three thousand miles away.”

“Twelve hundred from here to be exact. Don’t worry now. Consider it a road trip. The rest is up to you. You can take your load anywhere, but you can’t leave it here. And I have something else to ask of you. One last job...”

"This'll be fun, boys," Freebird said. They stood before a very large and very *green(?)* 1960s Mack RD600 Refuse Hauler. A tall and wide, malodorous behemoth, as grotesque as an armored dinosaur. Smelled like a garbage island and could probably haul a small town in its dustcart. Stenciled in large square letters on the side was ***~~Rocinante~~*** and below it, ***HULK SMASH!***

The storage facility on the hilltop overlooked the crowds and festivities down in St. Bardo. In the distance the sound of country songs and Mariachis. Fireworks popped off.

"Texas is far, man." Phobos said.

"And you're a wanted man in several states," Chuck added. He twisted and squirmed in his drunkenness.

"Change of plans," Freebird said. "This is a solo sojourn for me. Once I'm there I'll hire some migrants to help me. In the meantime, I have another job for you two."

Billy daKid showed up with a rugged earth mover, scooping the frozen contents out of cold storage and then pouring them into the dustcart.

Phobos scratched his messy beard. "What happens when they thaw out? You're going to be dripping water across several state lines."

"Garbage juice, my man," Freebird said. "Nobody questions garbage juice. No worries, no hurries."

"When's the last time you did a long haul?" Chuck said.

"That one time we drove all night to New Jersey to do the cleanup in Asbury Park."

"Geez. You sure about this?"

"Look at this beauty. She stinks but she's fucking strong. A classic. Nice of St. Bardo to loan her to me."

"What's this job you got for us?" Phobos said.

"You're not driving back to ATL just yet," Freebird said. "Some kids need a lift out of town. Nephew of St. Bardo and his girlfriend, or some chick. Here's cash for gas. You're to drive them to West River. You know, the coast?"

"I know where it is. We were just there. But I don't know what this is all about. Driving some kids to the beach? They having a picnic?"

"I don't know, okay?" Freebird said, and cracked his neck. "It's Bardo's family, you're driving them to where they need to go. That's it. You can go wherever the fuck you want to after you drop them off. Hey, somebody get me coffee for the road."

Half an hour later Billy daKid brought him coffee. Freebird backed the giant truck out of the parking lot as Phobos directed him. It was already dripping garbage juice from the seams. Phobos could see his muscular arm dangling out of the side window, his bearded face reflected in the long mirror. He looked calm. At task. The lot was gravel and the heavy truck struggled to back into the narrow street. Once he pulled out, he whistled Phobos over.

"Where's Chuck?" Freebird said.

"Passed out in the Caddy."

"Get there in one piece. Don't argue. Do what they say."

"Okay. They better play nice though."

"I'll see you in a week, give or take."

"How's your manifest?"

"Clean. It's garbage, right? It's a garbage truck. I've got contacts between here and there. Might even get a Smokey escort. Maybe head down to Mexico for tacos and margaritas after."

"You sound like a man with a plan."

"That's why I always win, Phobos. Don't forget to tell St. Bardo goodnight. Wish him a happy birthday. Cheer at the titties. That's a big thing around here. Don't forget, generous gratuity where applicable. I wouldn't recommend staying here too long, though."

"Why?"

"Trust me. It'll entice you, and give you access to fun things, and lots of vices, but it gets old fast."

"I kind of like the clowns and jugglers, though."

Phobos backed away, waving. Freebird flashed the peace sign and drove off. The truck shivered and coughed but picked up speed. It took Freebird about two days to get there, but that's another story.

Phobos got to the Great White and found Chuck asleep. There were three shadows in the backseat. People he didn't know. People wearing Halloween make-up and holding guns.

One wore clown makeup with a red bulbous nose. Another wore a Viking helmet like a cartoon opera singer, and their leader was a bald, horned *madhatter* with a waxed mustache and a slanted gaze. He wore a monocle and held a miniature pitchfork. There was a .45 in his other hand. The others had weapons too.

Fireworks burst above them.

"I guess you're the crew," Phobos said. "Where are we going?"

"Get in. Sit down," the madhatter said, adjusting his top hat. His horns poked through the holes in the stovepipe.

Phobos obeyed. He got in, switched on the light.

The madhatter said,

"My name is Pony St. Trash, the Pope of Irony. You can just call me Trash. Make yourself comfortable. It's going to be a long ride. Switch off your taxi light. Get on the highway and let's leave Clown Town to the clowns. Drive."

"Isn't there anyone else you can ride with?" Phobos said. "Kind of tired. Been driving all day."

"We're going to the coast, my good man. I was told you're the best driver to get us there." Trash feigned a weak-sounding, mock British accent. "We'll stop for coffee, and palaver with the dead along the way. We'll try not to get your car too dirty."

"Do you have to keep your guns out? I'm not driving getaway for you. If you think that's what I'm going to do you can get the fuck out of this car right now."

"Relax, curly. I'll do no such thing. We're separatists, we're nihilists, we're Stalinists. Second Amendment fetishists. We're just headed to another party on the east coast. Hang out with some friends, smoke a lot of weed, do a lot of drugs. Go on. *Drive!* We are on our way to start a revolution. *Go baby, go!*"

Chuck was still passed out when Phobos got the car moving. The country roads were dark, but he found the highway and its blurry signs.

Yesterday.

"I just want to kiss all the dogs," K-Less said. She clawed viciously at her pubic hair through her jeans. She sat in the passenger seat leaning back, smoking a very thick blunt that smelled like a burning chemical toilet. "I want to kiss all of them, let them slobber on my face, make-out with them, jack-off their lipstick dicks."

Late night, when all the roads were empty. The van traveled southwest from Virginia. Urban drove. He was a hulk of a black man under a knitted hat, hugging the wheel while roasting his own grotesque blunt. Falling asleep at the controls.

"Urb, you're zigging and zagging," Trash said. He recalled meeting him in the back of a health food restaurant months ago. Wannabe-Rasta prophet wearing a knitted cap, smoking a fat blunt like he was now.

"Been driving since last night," Urban said. "It's your van. Why don't you come up here and takeover?"

Trash sat between two giggling women who wore ghoulish clown makeup and babbled through plastic vampire fangs. One of them wore a Viking helmet with horns.

"I'm just getting started," Trash said. He lit a joint the size of a femur. "*I need this.* I need this."

K-Less had the most miserable melted frown Trash had ever seen. She squirmed in her seat, twitchy and itchy. He winced when she swiveled her chair to look at him.

"Where are the masks?" Urban said. When he wasn't taking a toke, he was chewing gum, or rubbing his eyes.

"Don't need 'em," Trash said. "We have makeup artists with us."

"That's messed up, man. Look at you all! Why don't we get to put on masks?"

"It's not that kind of scene, man. Everyone involved knows each other. This is who we are. Don't appropriate our culture! We're all friends here. What do you have to worry about?"

"Because they can pick me out of a thousand lineups if that was the case I caught. And you know the first one to go is always the Rasta nigga."

"I've known you for a minute, Urb. And I don't know where you're from. I can't place you. Your accent. New York? Boston? Chicago?"

"Nah, man. Philly."

"Ah, right on, brother. *Brother*."

"Where the guns?"

"They're stashed."

"You got one with you. Why don't we?"

"You know how hard it is to get a piece in them northern states? I'll distribute them when we get to where they're stashed. *Real* ammunition. But that's later. *After* the job."

Urban took a deep breath and grunted. He sounded like a waking dragon. Smoke emanated from his throat like a roasting hearth. "Why do we have to wait on Terry?"

"Because he's the man with the keys." Trash said. "See why we don't really need guns *right now,* Urb?"

"We're revolutionaries. We're taking what's rightfully ours. And he's just got keys? What kind of show is this?"

"You'll get plenty of time to flex, brother. And are you sure the payroll we're taking is yours? Because it's not. It's the people's payroll."

"Hey, they getting paid anyway. We're just taking the advance from the pig hierarchy." Urban grabbed an empty brown bottle from the dashboard and shook it. He dropped it on the floor.

"We outta gravy," K-Less said. She had a round flat face and sleepy eyes. Hairy legs stretched out, dirty feet on the dash. "God, can we pull over?"

"Why?" Urban said.

"This tampon's clogging me up. Gotta yank it."

"Can't stop now, girl. Ain't no place to stop."

"If you don't stop, I'm going to pull it out right here and throw it out the window!"

One of the ghoulish clowns in the back laughed. *"Give a hoot, don't pollute!"*

"We gonna split after we're done," Urban told Trash. "Go separate ways."

"I'm escaping to a forest," K-Less said.

"Don't say that so loud, girl. Don't give yourself away like that."

Trash cleared his throat. "Did you forget we're going to West River to talk with Koi and The Professor?"

"Ahh," Urban palmed his forehead. "Shit. Okay then. We'll regroup there. You heard that, baby girl? First things first."

K-Less snorted, *"But I wanna go see the trees first."*

Sharedale was a small town. Desolate at this time of night. The old plaza would soon host a batch of new box stores and fast food squares. The lights in parking lot were bright, the pavement slick from a recent rain. The van parked in the middle of it. Urban turned off the engine and faced them. K-Less rolled down her window and spit. She snuffed out the half-smoked bazooka she'd been sucking on and tucked it between her breasts.

"I got something for you." Urban gave them all a hard stare. They could only see one of his eyes as his hat covered most of his face. He grabbed a box at his feet and opened it. He tossed little bundles of t-shirts at each of them.

Trash gave his ladies a sideways leer.

"Go ahead," Urban said. "Try them on, motherfuckers."

Trash bent over and picked his off the floor. The others unfolded theirs, measured them against their chests. The shirts were green and sported a fist emblem with a red star in the middle, and the word *Stalling!* inscribed underneath.

"Um," Trash said.

The ladies giggled.

"Well," Urban said. "Put them on."

"Urb," Trash said. "The other day I was in Pennsylvania. You know that I've gone everywhere to draft as many participants as possible for our cause. The other day, I was traveling on SEPTA, and I overheard this man telling a small circle of listeners that holding in your piss gives you diabetes. You believe that shit?"

"Well, maybe it does." Urban said.

"It does not. It. Does not. Everywhere you go, in any city you go, there are corner preachers speaking to the lowly ones at their feet. Crazy makes prophets out of anyone, anywhere. Makes us all *prognosticators*. Or just really good liars. Good *jive turkeys*."

Urban stared, fuming. Maybe he really was a dragon under the hat and heavy military jacket.

"I made those shirts," Urban said. "You ain't gonna wear them?"

"This isn't a family reunion-barbecue, brother." Trash said. "Drive the van around to the back door. Terry will be here shortly to let us in. He'll probably be here in his family wagon. He's got kids now, family, the whole shit."

Urban parked beside an overflowing dumpster.

"Oh shit," one of the girls with Trash said. "There's a camera over the doorway."

"Terry says they don't bother turning them on," Trash said. "Just the ones over the cash registers so they can catch the workers stealing."

The five of them got out of the van and rested against the concrete wall. Posing like an album cover.

"Yo, gimme a gun," Urban said.

Trash looked at him. "We're not going in with guns. We're going into the payroll office. There's no one inside. They don't have overnight security."

"Let me hold yours." Urban said. "Just in case."

"Can I go buy cigarettes?" K-Less said.

"Right now?" Urban said.

"Don't worry, it'll be a minute before Terry gets here," Trash said. He looked at Ghoul Girl. "Go with her."

Ghoul Girl nodded. Trash looked into her eyes and she knew.

K-Less skipped off, smelling of oil and cigarettes. Ghoul Girl followed. Trash watched them go up the middle of the parking lot to the boulevard. A scraggly hippie and a plump velvet vampire walking side by side.

"Come on, man." Urban said. "The gun. It's right there in your belt."

"Hey, man. Chill the fuck out. You won't need it."

Urban reached over and grabbed it from him and tucked it into his own pants.

"You happy now?" Trash said. A car was approaching. A small family wagon.

"Man, this piece is held together with tape," Urban said. It was the last thing he said before he saw Terry walking towards the building.

Terry was a husky black man still in his managerial clothes. His armpits and forehead were sweaty. He reeked of the cologne used to cover it up.

"What's up, my man?" Trash said, twirling his mustache between his thumb and forefinger. "You all right? Look like you just ran the Big Mac relay."

"Ha, motherfucker." Terry said. Secret handshakes, sweaty hugs. "Man, I was just in my part of town, decided to rob this guy at the cash machine."

"Yeah?" Urban said.

"Was he a white capitalist?" Trash said.

"Shit, I don't know," Terry said. "Like I give a fuck. He was scared of me so I shook him down. Didn't even have a gun with me or nothing. Motherfuckers see a black juggernaut coming and they're shit-scared. Gotta flex so they know I ain't nothin' to fuck wit. Just 'cause I'm in the corporate world now, don't mean I ain't gonna rob a motherfucker."

"You damn right," Trash said. "*Get whitey*."

Terry unlocked the heavy metal door and went in quickly to shut off the alarm. He came back out and held the door open.

"But they're gonna know somebody let us in." Urban said going into the dark warehouse.

"Nah," Terry said. "The closing manager is this old senile dude who sometimes forgets to set the alarm at night. He'll take the fall. He's close to retiring anyway. Go straight to the front. Safe's open."

Half a mile away, walking the edge of the boulevard was K-Less and Ghoul Girl. Cars and buses honked at them.

"Are you his girlfriend?" K-Less said.

"Not really," Ghoul Girl said. "I'm just his sub."

"Is that clown chick your sister?"

"Sometimes. Are you and the black guy going together?"

"No way. I mean, I don't have anything against dating blacks. We just fuck. We're poly."

A car honked. Someone yelled, *"Show your tits!"*

K-Less put her hand down her shorts, yanked out her plug and flung it at the passing car.

"I've dated all sorts of people though," she said. "Blacks, whites, Mexicans, Asians, lesbians, transgendered, pre-op trans, you know. Whomever. *Whatever*."

"Uh huh."

"You got any coke?"

"No."

They bought cigarettes and walked back.

"I guess the robbery is in session," K-Less said.

"Yup," said Ghoul Girl. "And the revolution begins *now*."

"I need some coke first, though."

A gunshot rang from the plaza where the van was parked.

K-Less stopped. "I thought they weren't using guns."

"Uh huh," Ghoul Girl stood next to her. When she saw the oncoming bus, she shoved K-Less into traffic. Her head smashed the big windshield, her left leg got caught under the bus's right front tire, and then the bus ate her.

Ghoul Girl cut across the long parking lot toward the van.

Minutes before, three of them had come out of the warehouse with bags of money. One bag each. Very small bags. Terry locked up and drove off without another word.

"Man, this is it?" Urban said.

"It's a start," Trash said. He opened the van doors.

"That's busted, man. Nah. Hold up."

When Trash looked back, Urban was pointing the gun at his face.

"I'm just gonna have to take those," Urban said. He pulled back the hammer. Clown Girl got pushed onto the van and got her bag snatched.

"Okay," Trash said. "You drive. The revolution happens with or without you. What are you going to do with the funds? Jesus. It's like Che in the Congo."

"The fuck is you talking about?"

"Don't you want to wait for your girl to comeback?"

"Man, fuck that hoe. And you too." Urban pulled the trigger, but the rackety gun exploded in his hand. He howled and fell to his knees. Trash drew a gun from the back of his pants and pointed it at his face.

"Silence him," he said and the clown-faced girl went down on Urban with her daggers drawn. When Ghoul Girl returned with cigarettes, she joined in.

“What’s in the briefcase?” Danielle said.

“Don’t worry about it.” The Professor said. “Was there anyone following us?”

“My rearview is broken. If I turn my head to look, I’m bound to crash.”

“What city is this?”

“We just drove through Southside. We’re heading toward Rome.”

“The coast is behind us?” The Professor said.

“Far behind us,” said Danielle. “No beach, no water near us right now. There’s a creek up past the dump, but you can’t swim in it.”

“Where are you taking me?”

“There’s a medic in Rome. She fixed my dog once. Works out of her home. He’s long gone now, but she worked her magic on him and he lived many years.”

“I’m not a dog.”

“She’s not beyond removing a random bullet. It looks like I picked the perfect time to leave town.”

“Why didn’t you call the police or an ambulance?”

“You think I can trust them? Because I don’t. And you look like somebody who shouldn’t trust them. I didn’t want you to get in trouble.”

“How do you know I’m in trouble?”

“You were a stranger passing through. Gibton is like the old west, gunfights happening all the time. Meth Mafia shootouts on the weekend. I was waiting for a sign to leave so I left. I won’t miss it. Nobody’s going to miss me.”

"Well, at least you're not a meth head."

"No. I don't want to lose my teeth. That happened to my cousin Lara."

"Look, that's all good and all." The Professor said. "I mean, sorry about your cousin. I appreciate it but you didn't have to get involved. I have some things of value that people want. You ever heard of a rapper named Boots Tumbler?"

"Not particularly," Danielle said. "I don't really listen to rap all that much. I'm a country girl. I like Reba. I love her songs. And Britney."

"No matter. I no longer know who's on my side. Forget I asked."

"How'd you get shot?"

"It's a sketchy story. I can feel the bullet right there in my side. If I haven't mentioned it: I'm grateful for what you've done."

“Before we get much further,” Trash said. “We need to make a stop and raise the dead. What's that cemetery called?”

“I don’t know,” Clown Face said. She no longer wore the red clown nose but had the glee of a psychotic kindergartener. Wide sad eyes, and the tiniest mouth. There was an old hag face sagging behind the makeup.

“Anyway, *driver*,” Trash said. “the first cemetery you see off the road. That’s the one. Stop at that one. You have a shovel in this car?”

Phobos looked through the rearview. “Yeah. Maybe. What for?”

“In case we need a dirt nap. If not, use your hands.”

The pitch-black country road lit up with the Great White’s headlights. Phobos stepped on it and took a sharp curve that led to a shortcut. The Great White barreled forward, plowing over greenery like manifest destiny until it was back on the main county road. They sped past an abandoned conversion van parked under a tree. Doors opened, interior gutted.

Trash waved at it. “Bye-bye, baby.”

“Um gonna miss her,” Ghoul Girl said.

Trash to Phobos: “Turn the light on in here. I can’t see.”

Through the rearview, Phobos watched the madhatter pull up a crumbled bag.

“Would you boys care for a shmoke?” Trash said.

“Not while I’m driving, man.” Phobos said. “And I’d rather you wouldn’t smoke up the car. It’s not mine.”

“You’re missing out, man. This stash is a mind-cruncher. Transatlantic super homo-sapien angel flight horns of Gabriel across a universe of sand and stars, and limp elephants. That's what this is. This is what's going to start our revolution."

"You guys farm cannabis?" Phobos said. "I thought of doing that. Might move to Denver and get that started. This guy I know just moved out there."

"We don't grow," Trash said. "We remix. We add our secret herbs and spices, and then we *share*. Do a little magic and then puff-puff. Regular *Dungeons & Dragons* but with Marxism and fisticuffs."

"And guns," Ghoul Girl said.

Black was the night. They drove an hour in silence. Trash had taken out one of his giant joints and smoked some of it by himself. He cackled and growled.

"Try it, man." Trash said.

Phobos shook his head.

"As your co-pilot," Trash said. "I advise you to try some. A few pulls is all you need."

"It's cool, man," Phobos said. "Don't really feel like it when I'm driving."

Trash pointed the joint at his head. "Come on, man."

The joint smelled like roasting hay and burning plastic. Trash wasn't sharing with the girls. There were laughs, there were giggle-fits.

Phobos said, "I was in a rehab program recently on account that I almost died of a heroin overdose. I don't touch substances anymore. Maybe weed but that's it."

"This is weed, goddammit! It's pure, grown in dirt." Trash said.

"No, man. I've been around enough dust-heads to know your shit is laced."

"What?" Trash feigned shock. "Never!"

"I don't know what it's laced with, but I don't want it."

"What about your sleeping friend there?"

"Nah. No thanks." Phobos said. "How are you going to ruin something that's natural and comes from the earth?"

"Come on, *Mr. Natural.* Don't be a quitter," Trash said. "We'll get there faster if you smoke it."

"That's like, more of a hippie-zombie thing. You guys look like a bunch of revolutionary goth punks."

"Labels are for losers, *loser.*" Trash took a long drag and blew smoke at the Ghoul Girl and Clown Face.

Ghoul Girl with her spooky mutant face, like the cherubic young sister of Morticia Addams, cocked her gun and put it at Phobos' neck.

"Pull over," she said. She was the first to spot the tombstones. "I want to dance on some graves."

"Hold on," Phobos said. He let the Great White cruise a bit until it reached the entrance to the cemetery and then turned into it.

"It's going to be a long night. You better get used to it," Clown Face said.

"Crank up the radio," said Ghoul Girl. "Something loud."

Nightmare River...

Signs for open trails appeared at every mile marker. Trash kept pointing and sniffing out ghosts that puffed and then left in a vapor cloud.

"Finally," he told Phobos. "Keep driving, motherfucker! *Yeahahahaha!*"

The road was oyster-shell gravel. It twisted, turned, and swirled around a patch of graves. At the center was a small mausoleum with a single bench between two concrete pillars.

The throne lit up with the Great White's car lamps. The path around the graves was overgrown. The night felt still and desolate. But the trees were alert with the incessant grind of chirping insects. Occasionally an owl hooted.

Trash jumped out before the car stopped, arms close to his chest, clawing like a tyrannosaurus rex on its last run. He howled like a wolf and then tumbled, rolled and wound up on his feet holding his gun like a Boy Scout combatant. The Ghoul and the Clown followed him, carefully reading every headstone, jumping over graves, or ungracefully rolling over them, and then landing flat and pretending to be dead. Humping graves, and stroking the crosses.

"Tra la loo loo loo..." Ghoul Girl said. She twirled and danced with surprising grace. "This is what it'll be like when I go. I want to get married at my funeral."

"I told you before," Trash said. "The presence of ghosts don't guarantee your immortality. It don't prove there's an ever-after life-eternal! Your morbid curiosity only means you're a pure Narcissist in the worst kind of way."

"Whatever," she said. "You read too much *Ram-boh.*"

Phobos parked the car, woke up Chuck, and they sat on the hood. They watched their shadows traipse among the gravestones. Creeping through splintered moonlight into the dreamland of the dead.

At some point Trash stopped the monkey antics to smell the air. He held his head high and sniffed. There was a mound of crushed cinderblocks and he made the two women crawl over it erotically. Then he went to the concrete throne and sat in it. He contemplated like Rodin's *Le Penseur*, then got on his knees and slid the heavy seat toward by himself. The concrete rumbled with a guttural burp.

"Behold, there be treasures!" Trash said. He clicked a small flashlight from his keychain. In the box under the throne was the left half a human skull, some bone trinkets, feathers, old candles, two machine guns and a few handguns and clips. And a bottle of formaldehyde. He passed out the guns, the half-skull and the trinkets, and then embraced the bottle close to his chest. He slid the concrete cover back in its place.

"Is that some kind of hooch?" Phobos said.

Trash posed with the chemical bottle, caressing its side like it was fine wine. "It is *some* kind of hooch."

"I'd like for you to stash those weapons in the trunk if you plan on bringing them." Phobos said.

"Nope," said Trash. "These are carry-ons."

"So, you're just gonna swing those guns around while we're on the highway?"

"No one's going to notice." Ghoul Girl said. She disrobed, so ghostly and pale, her blue veins pulsed with an orgonite glow. Every time she ran past the front of the car, she pointed the machine gun at them, making *pew* and *pow* noises with her mouth.

Phobos and Chuck stood on the edge of a quarry behind the mausoleum where the earth had broken off during a mudslide, forming a deep chasm. In the dawn's bleak ambience, they stared down into the abyss.

"You can pee-pee off there if you want, boys. Just don't fall in." Trash marched around cackling madly, pointing the small machine gun at them. Then he placed his feet right at the drop edge with his back to the chasm, pretending to lose his balance. The machine gun swung up and down as he rocked forward and back. The joint dangled from his bottom lip. Clown Face walked past him and snatched it. She sucked it in and then gave it to Ghoul Girl.

"Watch where you point that." Chuck told Trash. He pressed against Phobos, half-asleep. "Dude, they're fucking crazy. Where are we going?"

"The coast, I guess." Phobos said.

Ghoul Girl marched up behind them. She giggled to the point of hysteria.

"Kind of my favorite place, here." She said. "I love it."

"You done with that?" Trash grabbed the joint from her grip and danced around some more.

"So," Ghoul Girl said. Her velvet and vinyl were soaked with sweat. She smelled like a thrift store and day-old butter. "Why hasn't someone dug up a skeleton and danced with it?"

"Or fucked it!" Clown Face said. "Trash, tell these boys to dig one up. They look like gravediggers."

"Now, wait a minute." Chuck sat up.

"They'll do nothing of that sort," Trash said. He let his weapon dangle from his shoulder. Looking at both his hands, he said, "I don't really know what's become of us. I used to come out here years ago, when I was a teenager. Smoking weed, listening to folk music, and wiggling my naked ass into the creek below. Now look where I am. It's the flipside to paradise. All of this is so dark, dank, and dirty. Like me. I guess I've come full circle, Nightmare River."

During the quieter moments Phobos and Chuck glanced at each other.

"I gotta meet up with Boots tomorrow," Chuck said.

Phobos nodded.

The Stalinist trio froze up, lost in ecstatic paralysis but then slowly slid back into reality. Whatever they'd smoked coursed through them with raging toxicity. Trash rubbed his face and roared, then randomly shot his gun into the air. Ghoul Girl pointed her greasy machine gun at Phobos and Chuck. Her face was a bruised moon as she stood in the headlights.

Ghoul Girl cackled like an ancient, arctic witch:

"We came out here to dance. I told you fuckers to dance!"

Phobos went inside the car and turned up whatever was in the tape deck. Fleetwood Mac, "Coming Your Way".

Chuck immediately broke into a routine he only did when he was really drunk. Pop-locking, waving one arm and passing it to the other, except his other wasn't as receptive as it once was. Phobos stood next to the car doing a spastic forward and backward motion, rocking his head side-to-side, throwing in some de-syncopated hand motions.

Ghoul Girl sprayed the ground with bullets. "*That's what I want!* That's exactly what I want!"

"See?" Clown Face said. "No one got shot. *Losers.*"

Trash joined their dance from the edge of the quarry. He lifted his arms dramatically as if to conduct the crickets and mosquitos into a harmonious symphony.

"Oh no!" he said, feigning a British accent. He fell forward, rolled over and flattened out on the grass. He looked up at the stars and began to drool. He watched Phobos and Chuck dance. He saw Ghoul Girl and Clown Face caress and rock their guns like newborns. He fell into the suffocating darkness of space.

"Somebody, somebody please get me Koi Pond on the phone," Trash said. *"Tell him we're coming!"*

Their wide-eyed dreams were of tigers tearing off their faces and ripping them limb from limb.

When The Professor returned to life his head rocked forward and he suddenly woke with an aching side, but no longer bleeding.

"Good afternoon," Danielle said. "For a second, I thought you were dead. I was about to leave you at the side of the road."

He looked down at his blood-soaked suit.

"It would have been appropriate." His throat cracked. "They're after me. They'll catch up."

"Oh, there's no one following us. Don't worry. We've been on this road all day, and we're the only ones on it."

He noticed for the first time, other than her soothing voice, she had silky blonde hair, and a big smile. Pretty face. There was a gentle nimbus around her. She looked like she'd been cut and pasted from another scene, just hovering over her seat. An angel at the wheel.

"I've heard it said before, we all got demons to contend with," she said.

"If only. After a fierce bidding war, they decided to come after me and my wares. From all sides. Gun carrying, walking assassins. I don't know how many, but they've given pursuit."

"Sounds terrifying."

"Maybe I'm a little paranoid." The Professor said. "Some of them were my students, some were clients. They're all batshit insane and want my formula."

"You look like a professor," she said.

"A chemist, actually. I taught courses at EU. I was working to improve the world through mind-altering chemistry. They didn't care for that."

"I could never remember that periodic chart."

"You'd be surprised how often I have to argue science in this day and age. It's really about getting to know your elements down to their amino acid basics."

She droned and he faded her out, a scarecrow in his ruffled blood suit. His once white shirt that was now saturated red and pink, matching the color of his checkered tie. The handle of his briefcase was deep in his sweaty grip, permanently lodged there.

"I need to charge my phone." The Professor said. He tried his best to sit up straight but the pain returned.

"I'm sorry," Danielle said. "I don't have a charger. It's an old car anyway so you wouldn't be able to."

"I see that."

The radio didn't work, in fact it was missing. Gum had clogged up the air vents. There was a hairbrush on the floor entangled with blonde hair. McDonald's trash littered the backseat and floor. The door handle was greasy with what was either lip balm or Vaseline. He licked it off his fingers out of curiosity. It tasted like strawberry. The lysergic flow in his bloodstream was steadying. He had control of it now. Absentmindedness was a side-effect.

"Have you always lived in that town?" He said.

"I was born in Florida, but my mom moved us to Gibton. My brother, sister and me."

"I see." He was pale again, sweating and drawing short breaths but very much in the now, alive as he could be. His left hand was caked where blood had streamed and dried. "What do you think is out there waiting for you in the real world?"

"Gibton is the real world," she said. "A messed-up version of it. I know not all cities are just meth labs and video stores."

"I got news for you, sweetie. And I don't mean condescension when I say that. You're a real sweet kid. Genuine. Beautiful person. *But, there's nothing out there.* You must bring the whole picnic with you when you're stepping out to see the world. Otherwise, nothing happens."

"That's a little pessimistic, don't you think, Professor? Why'd you wind up there?"

"I went looking for a place to hide out, build a lab. I got shot. You know, kids and their guns these days. Then I drove my car into a pole. Now I'm here."

"We're just a hundred miles from Rome."

"I don't know that place." He said. His entire left side throbbed.

"Near Atlanta."

"Better be a good doctor for you to drive all this way."

"She is. And I'm just going to keep going after I leave you there. I'm not looking back. This is it for me."

"It's best you don't keep hanging around unsavory types. Me included."

"You're not unsavory. And not everyone in Gibton is unsavory. They're just...bored."

"Did you say goodbye to your family?"

"I'll call my mom."

"Was it something I said? Where do you think you'll go? Don't say California."

"I don't know. The desert, maybe. Never driven past the Mississippi."

"I'm going to doze off for a bit now."

"I hope you don't die in my car."

"I'd like to reward you for your help, but I'm tapped out at the moment."

"Don't worry about it, sir."

"The most valuable thing I have is my brain. And I can't part with it right now."

The Plumber wore a short beige coat. From his Spring/Summer collection. Sitting like a catalogue spread on a crowded public bus. His matching tool satchel was more of an elaborate carpet bag. He was the only white man onboard but casually non-descript. Eyes watching everything behind dark sunglasses. His hair was full and curly but very neat. He'd perfected his method of fitting in, where he was seen but otherwise ignored. Unlike his competitor, El Alacran, who had perfected invisibility.

His stop was Downtown, and he was the only passenger to get off there, elbowing his way off the bus. He boarded a train heading east, not used to traveling evenings. Finding some seclusion in an empty section of the car, he opened the tool satchel and took inventory. Large monkey wrench that once belonged to his father; a brand-new hacksaw, a small mallet, a U.S. Marine combat knife with a leather handle, leather gloves, a long PVC elbow pipe, duct tape, etc.

He thought about the competition that evening. Invisible men floating in and out of the city, hitting their miscellaneous marks. Business was thriving and he'd been pulled out of retirement because of demand. His week was fully booked, and he was glad to be traveling. The Plumber understood that each *independent contractor* had their own specialty and technique. It was all just hatchet work anyway. And any method used to finish the job was good enough. He didn't fuss over it. He rested his eyes as the train rocked steadily from station to station. It was past his bedtime.

Phobos drove southeast toward a beautiful sunrise.

A nimbus of sunlight encircled Trash's face. Ghoul Girl and Clown Face slept on his chest, guns pointing at his groin. Chuck buzzsawed with his head tilted back against the headrest.

Their silence was blissful. An hour later, Chuck continued his conversation with Phobos.

"I didn't know what was waiting for me," Chuck said. "But when I got there, he expected me to clear a mountain of shitty diapers from his backyard."

"Just piled up like that?" Phobos said leaning on his elbow. Right hand on the wheel.

"Dude, when I say mountain, I'm talking *Kilimanjaro*. His wife just balled them up and threw them out the window. And after I was done and had them all in my sister's truck, you know how much he paid me? Five bucks! Five fucking dollars to haul a ton of shitty diapers."

"How old were you?"

"Twelve."

"Fuck that," Phobos said. "I've been desperate. But I never hauled a mountain of shitty diapers for five dollars."

"Freebird was talking to me about a possible promotion." Chuck said softly.

The clowns in the back woke up and carried on with their stupidity. Poking each other, giggling, smoking.

"Aren't you supposed to be retired?" Phobos said.

"I'm thirty-seven," said Chuck. "I'm at the top of my game. Just looking for a better position with Freebird. Or get with a better outfit."

"I'm not sure that any of these 'outfits' are much organized these days. It's not like in the movies. It's all just loose and chaotic criminal bullshit."

"How so?"

"Total corporate mentality. More bosses than workers. Too many chiefs. Not knowing what to do with all the territory or all the product. Now they're at each other's throats competing like burger joints. 'Outfits' aren't holding up their end. Enforcers and mules care even less because they're not getting paid what they deserve. They're flaking out. Double crossing. Dying."

"I need to get with an Italian or Cuban syndicate," Chuck said. "They get shit done. Great benefits too."

"No such thing. Not in this state or the Carolinas. The only real gangsters here are in government offices. You wanna work for Cubans and Italians, you have to move to Florida."

"It's too fucking hot down there. But come on, dude. You've been around. You know the kind of work we do. The *people* we know."

Phobos pushed back his glasses. "Anything resembling organized crime here in the south is just end-of-the-world militias trafficking meth. Or black hustlers selling weed and bricks. Cubans have Miami. Italians don't want to live in the south. What can Italian mobsters organize here? To start with, there aren't any good Italian restaurants here."

"How about Morelli's on the South End?" Chuck said.

"He's Romanian and sells noodles with ketchup. I make better spaghetti out of a can."

"This is bullshit work."

"You never complained before. What do you think you're going to get with a new 'outfit'? We're sub-subcontractors. We're bottom guys."

"Can a man ever be truly satisfied? Right now, we're playing party bus for these creeps. There's options out there. How about the city of Carbon? Ever heard of Carbon? It's north of Jacksonville. There's an area they call The Humps. A *disposal* area."

"Hitchhiked through there once." Phobos spit out the window. "Got my ass beat. Almost got killed. It's so dirty you can never quite get the smell out of your beard."

Trash highjacked their conversation.

"Carbon is like a holiday in Cambodia, circa 1969." He said. "That's where the real pipe-hitters go. You should have included me in your morning chat. We could have planned something. We're all family now, right? Don't go fucking up my tribe vibe."

"Thought you were sleeping," Phobos said.

Trash rolled his eyes, leaned back and stretched. Phobos looked at Chuck.

"You talked me into this," he said.

Chuck shrugged. "Like I was saying, what the fuck else are we gonna do? Get office jobs? Pour coffee at some yuppie place like a pair of chumps?"

Phobos nodded.

"I want my grow-house back," Chuck said. "I was living all cozy and comfortable before I lit it."

"I don't care where I live." Phobos said. "I'm okay with the farm and the cats and the broken tractors. I can't seem to stay in one place for too long though."

“Maybe we can drive through Carbon when we’re done.” Trash said.

“That’s not happening,” Phobos said. “You can shoot me right now and throw me out the window, but that’s not happening.”

The Professor opened his eyes. Sun was setting but it wasn't dark yet. Cooler temperatures than earlier. He took in a quick breath and realized he was still alive. Sort of.

"Thought you'd shipped out again," Danielle said.

"I think I did. For a while. Dreamt of the beach. And dog fights. Very turbulent shit. What do you dream about?"

Danielle pressed back against her seat, arching and stretching. Her eyes widened, trying to make sense of the road ahead.

"Oh, I don't know," she said. "Normal stuff."

"How long have we been driving?"

"Few hours. I wasn't keeping track. We crossed a bridge and left everything back there."

"Were you daydreaming?"

"Sometimes. I'm more concerned with what's ahead, trying to stay out of the clouds. I don't really fantasize a lot. It's distracting. I'm in the moment mostly. Thinking straight ahead. Thinking I have to call my sister Angela and tell her that I left."

"Tell me about Angela."

"She still lives in Gibton. In a trailer. Well, I lived in a trailer too. I moved out from her place a while back. She's older than me and had a good trajectory. She was good in school and all. But mom got sick and Angela had to help out. She lost her virginity to her boss at the Rite Aid. Threw away her scholarship when she got pregnant by that pencil-dick redneck. I've never liked him and he's like twenty years older than her. She just got fat and had a bunch of kids she neglected. I love her and see them on Christmas but that's not what I want to be around. I feel that maybe she made the sacrifice for me. She took the fall and now I get to escape. I've partied a little, did some modeling but truthfully, every man I meet is just flim-flam. And plus, I don't need a man to support or define me."

The Professor watched her as she spoke.

"Go on," he said. "That's brilliant of you. Do what you must."

"Watching you die has been inspiring. You think you'll make it?"

"I've stopped bleeding. Maybe I ran out of blood."

"We're almost there."

"I'm kind of numb right now. Very numb."

"You'll be better once you're looked at, and the wound is attended."

"I know I'm not dying. Because when I do eventually go, there'll be a fleet carrying me off to the River Styx. So, I'm not dead yet."

Of the 300 languages spoken in the U.S. he only spoke Spanish. Or so he led you to think. It didn't matter whether El Alacran was seen or how he blended in. Or what he spoke. He was invisible, and those who've seen him would swear he could walk through walls. He could certainly walk through people when he had to. Walk off a scorching road wearing a leather jacket, not even break a sweat. Nothing glamorous about him or how he went about his job.

Woke up early as possible to get to it. Showered and shaved. Dressed and departed. Wearing snakeskin boots, tight blue jeans, a neatly tucked collared shirt, and an aged leather jacket. Pants held up by a thick belt, clasped with a silver buckle. He smelled of Old Spice and leather. His mustache and neatly trimmed hairline and chops were a thing of architecture. Sunglasses and toothpick to accessorize. Only in town for a day or so, leaving no trace that he'd ever been here.

At a diner he sat in a booth by the far corner. He waited patiently. Ordered, ate his breakfast neatly. Never ordered the same thing twice nor ate at the same establishment more than once. And if he could avoid it, he never visited the same town twice. He paid in cash. Gone without anyone noticing he'd been there at all.

"In the future, privacy will be our greatest commodity." Blake, his administrator, had recently told him from behind a cloud of cigar smoke. "Once you're exposed, there's no hiding your face, or your address, or your dick from the rest of the world. Not these days when everything is right there on a device in the palm of your hand."

"I just float," El Alacran had said. He had a method of communicating by staring hard, and sometimes squinting.

Speaking was of little necessity.

The waitress was quaint, unassuming. Not in a hurry, got everything right. Didn't make a lot of conversation but smiled when pouring coffee and that was enough. El Alacran had multiple techniques for disconnecting from everyone and everything in the world and they all worked. When he reentered into the fold of the public, he knew he had to act like he was one of them. Had to feign kindness, courtesy, and exchanges, no matter how banal. Tip well, but don't over-tip. At the friendliest moment, pull out, leave through the back exit when available. Don't come back.

He says hello but no one hears him. He never says goodbye. They don't see him leave. He does all of this work with his hands so he carries only a small pair of black gloves made of thin leather. Easy to tuck into his jacket pocket. In his other pocket his razor-thin phone had rung. He'd floated across the city for a meeting with Blake. It was rare to ever see him come into the office. The man behind the smoke told him so.

"Usually, it's Matz who delivers the assignments. I don't blame you for being obscure. I am at least glad to see you have a portable phone where my assistant can reach you."

El Alacran nodded.

"I don't keep one myself, to be honest." Blake said. "But I understand. Lucky for you, you have a personal vendetta in this case. Because of what they did. You already know what they look like, who they are. Even after all these years, you are familiar with how they operate. I know they're on a different level, and that one of them is related to St. Bardo. While this move may cause a rift between the organizations, it is necessary. We can't have too many cowboys out there just shooting up the place and getting the spotlight shined back on all of us. Absolutely no way. They say they have a cause. No. We're going to nip that right now. What cause? Who's really starving? Who are they revolting against? The odds remain as they have been. No need to tip the scales. You're my balancing man. You know what to do."

El Alacran nodded.

"I mean what they did to your family and how they disposed of them."

El Alacran's eyes thinned and turned pure onyx, with which to see through steel and brick. With which to see the outline of an internal organ before he tears it out.

"You were patient and didn't move in on them until you got permission," Blake said. "This should be a piece of cake. I know you don't care for these details but by doing this, you're leveling off the playing field for everyone. I imagine you'll get some satisfaction of your own out of this, as your hands get a little dirty."

Blake's speech was so crisp and electric that the air crackled with static. "Where I come from, we pay all outstanding balances. And everybody, eventually, pays their tab. They've turned up again, after months of underground bombings, kidnappings, political hijackings. And the joke is on us, every time they run off with the ransom that's paid. They took years from your life, took your family, *your soul*, and you've waited and waited. Now they're playing like they're a bunch of circus freaks, and there is nothing worse than a bunch of trust fund kids with a political slant, shooting their way through our territory passing off their poison for recreational use. I imagine you'll have no regrets doing this."

"I never regret a thing."

"Well, then." Blake said. "That suffering made you a little dead on the inside. It'll be easy. Go to it. You've got your license for a spree. Do what you must and get it done."

Ghoul Girl poked Trash with the long barrel of her homemade gun. "Wake up," she said. "This ain't recess."

"Are we there?" Trash said, eyes half-shut. He placed his monocle over his right eye. The bottle of formaldehyde sat comfortably between his thighs. To his left, Clown Face was motioning her machine gun in the air, making airplane sounds.

Phobos sweated. Chuck snored.

The clogged multi-lane freeway looked like a parking lot. The orange sun was warped and runny between glass buildings. The three Stalinists had applied more clown makeup to each other. They smelled like sweaty leather, gun oil and dusty denim.

Chuck woke up, craned his head. "Fuck." He shut one eye and rubbed the top of his head. He looked back at them again. "Fuck. It's not even Halloween. Hey brother, don't you ever sleep?"

Phobos shook his head.

"Keep on truckin'." Chuck said.

"You should've smoked instead of getting so drunk." Ghoul Girl told him. "Now your head's gonna explode."

Chuck was captivated by her bright evil eyes and Raggedy Ann face. He said, "Not my first hangover, lady."

"I had a condo out here," Trash pointed to a glass building. "We'd rave it up on the roof, drop acid and hail Satan."

"Zombies!" Clown Face said, nauseatingly seductive.

"Correct." Trash said. "Aren't you glad I recovered this bottle? It ain't phencyclidine but it'll do. Can't you smell it? The trashman's cigar. Roll up a few and dip 'em. We'll pass them out at the party. The rest takes care of itself." He reached up and yanked Phobos by his headband. "Exit here."

"That's what I fucking smell." Chuck said. "You guys been smoking Sherm?"

"Amateur." Trash said. "Fuck you."

"I smoked that shit in sixth grade, poser." Phobos said.

"Yeah, poser," Chuck said. "Don't go offering that shit if people don't know it's tricked out."

"It's the generic kind," Trash said. "Phencyclidine is scarce in Bardo. My uncle don't allow it. We've had to improvise."

Ghoul Girl brought her mouth within an inch from Phobos' face and chomped the air. Then she stuck her out tongue and licked him. She looked back at Clown Face. "We were howling at the moon like zombie-wolves last night! Tonight's gonna be even crazier!"

The Great White took an offramp near a gas station and they all bought tall coffees. They drove up to the top deck of a parking garage. Trash shoved a mix tape into the car's deck and blasted out death metal. They got out and danced around. They smashed their bodies together, holding their coffee cups, guns, and poison cigars.

"The last time a stranger showed up from nowhere and changed my life was a man named Parker Willingham." Danielle said, making sure The Professor wasn't going to pass out for good. She wanted to jab him but was afraid he'd spring a leak.

"Never heard of him." The Professor said. "Was he a chemist?"

"No." She said. "Not at all. He told me he was a genius and I believed him."

"I certainly won't lie to you that way. Do you usually do such impulsive things? Like leave your town on short notice. I doubt I will change anything in your life."

Danielle agreed. "Maybe it's fate. I wouldn't be here at this very moment if you hadn't crashed your car in Gibton. Parker was a real, how do you call it, a *charlatan*? I met him when I was sixteen. He walked right into the video shop much like you did. That corner is a crossroad of sorts. People tend to blow right through with the wind and dust devils. He said he was a photographer looking for models. I was looking for a one-way ticket out of Gibton. I know I'm cute and my hair is nice, and I look good in jeans. So, we hung out a bit. Not like dating or anything. He didn't have any moves at all. He barely showed interest. Always bragged about only dating models or girls he said were prettier than me. We used to watch a lot of cheerleading practice videos in his trailer. That was his thing I guess but it didn't bother me none because he was too goofy and harmless. But he lied. Compulsively. I never saw any of his work. Only a few of the photos we did, you know, fashion stuff. But nothing ever came of it. He was all talk, all bullshit. Took me a year to realize that. He said he would change me. Change us all when his company went big. But he was just some stupid hick with a cheap camera. Phonies like him are everywhere in that town. He got mad when I signed up for college. He never even asked me on a proper date."

"I may be weird but I'm no phony." The Professor said.

"I don't think you are."

"A person can drive, and just disappear. No burial, no tears, no calls to Jesus. I'm more interested in not bleeding to death. You wanna try one of these? They dissolve right on your tongue."

"No, thank you." She said.

"All right. You can have a sheet if you want. I assure you it's premium lysergic acid. So, whatever became of him? The photographer."

"He met up with a few girls and he promised all of them a future and they fell for it. Like any hick girl from a meth town would. He had all these companies he created, and licensed. You know, like all this LLC? But they sold nothing. He had no product. Just bullshit. Endless bullshit. He made up stuff he wanted to do but never did it. The *bullshitting* was his biggest trick."

The Professor swiveled his body just so. "I've known many men like that, and perhaps I'm like that too. Mine was a quick experiment that got out of hand. But it's no trick. I'm sorry he fooled you. Sounds like a real a jerk. You should find him and kick his ass."

"I figure I'll just leave it behind. It's amazing what people fall for," she said. "Gibton is nothing. Full of nobodies. Last I heard he was trying to make motion pictures, but I haven't seen or talked to him in several years. That's why I mostly keep to myself these days."

"Keep on running then." The Professor said. "I don't think they'll take me back at the university. Ever. I've been judged and casted out. Terrorist cell organizer, drug chemist, drug pusher. I accidentally discovered this magical formula and was ostracized when I tried to share it with the world. I'm going to have to leave the country soon."

"I'll say this," she said. "I've come across outsiders, and fugitives that I've sent over this way. I don't know what became of them or where they went after she fixed them."

"Are you handing me over to be sacrificed?"

"I don't think so," she said.

"The devil would turn me away if we met."

"That's sad, Professor."

"Call me Karl." He said.

"Sure."

"And it's not sad. It just *is*."

"I get it."

While she focused on driving, he studied the roads. Nature had been compromised. Box buildings enveloped the landscape from one town to the next. Bigger billboards, bigger logos.

"When did I enter the picture?" he said cleaning his glasses. "I feel like I'm caught in a loop."

"How's that?"

"When did I actually walk into your life? Exactly at what point?"

"Well, you came into the video store earlier today, after about ten. You fell over my counter. I picked you up off the ground and cleaned you up a little. Now I'm trying to keep you from dying."

"I fell off the magic carpet."

"I'm sure you're still on it," she said. "People pass through Gibton all the time. To dump their garbage or buy meth."

"I ran when I should have stayed for dead." He panicked, squirming painfully in his seat. "Why am I here? Can your doctor really fix me? This was my doing. I manifested this wound. Are you taking me to the land of the dead? Across a purgatorial scape? Carrying me off to my canoe?"

Danielle reached over and felt his forehead with the back of her hand. He was shivering. While holding the wheel she dug into her purse and pulled out an orange prescription bottle and singlehandedly poured out a few pills and then scooped them into his mouth.

"Here," she handed him her warm soda and he obliged, swallowing hard and coughing.

"Not sure how this will mix." He said. Sweat poured down his temples.

"I don't either," she said. "They're my roommate's pills."

The Professor dozed off. He sprung awake a few minutes later.

"Are you sure that stuff you cooked up is safe?" Danielle said.

"It's keeping me alive. Most of my soul is still intact."

"You know how Indians believe that their souls get taken when they're photographed?"

"Most indigenous cultures share a similar superstition."

"That's how I felt when I posed for Willingham. Like my substance had been sucked out and I just couldn't find it or replace it. I didn't know what it was but I knew it was missing."

"Your innocence?" He said.

"My essence. I don't feel lost or out of sorts. I know something is missing though. I think he took it and fled with it. I may spend my future looking to get it back."

"It may not be what it was. I don't know you that well, but you're doing right by the universe. You have a friendly, pure demeanor. What were those pills? They eased the pain and increased my euphoria. Please don't let me fall asleep again. I like the jitters and highs when I avoid the sleepiness. Plus, I might die if I fall asleep again. If I haven't already."

Two-lane back country roads. Empty roadside shacks, creaking general stores abandoned years ago. Shortly after, condominiums and other new construction appeared.

New homes starting in the low $400's.

Staring at the sun, he said,

"Hey, how far are we from Mexico?"

"Far," she said. "Like real far."

"Feels like we've been driving for days. Funny how the concept of time deceives the ape. I suppose bleeding to death will also make you react that way."

"I can't drive to Mexico." She said. "I don't really want to go there. But I'm sure in Rome you might be able to grab a bus to anywhere. You thinking of just fucking-off everything?"

"Already have, honestly."

The Professor tried not to fade away.

The Professor was biting his lip when they came upon a property hidden behind banana trees and other leafy giants. The tunnel of vegetation was tight around the car as it drove toward the gate. Beyond the fence, was a humble modular home. The yard was a small zoo.

Danielle stopped the car in front of a zinc gate crowned with barbed wire. The words **STAY OUT!!** were hand painted neatly but with intent on a wooden placard.

The Professor's vision was smudgy, but he noticed a collapsed mobile home deep in the backyard. He remembered getting shot by the bubblegum kid and his side began to ache. The mobile home was abandoned, covered in moss. The roof had caved in and a small tree sprouted branches through the windows. The siding was a veneer of mushrooms growing in abstract patterns. Next to it was a fancy brown conversion van with dark tinted windows.

"Welcome to Dr. Jordan's plantation," Danielle said opening his door from the passenger side.

Looking at them from inside the gate was a black woman, felid eyes peering through the mail slot. Her hair was crimson red. Her face stoic and predatorial. A yellow snake coiled around her neck, and a reddish one around her left arm.

"The vet office is closed today," Nola hissed.

"Dr. Jordan, it's Danielle." She walked slowly to the gate, brushing aside the heavy vegetation. "This man is wounded. He's needs a bullet taken out of him."

"Don't come any closer." Nola said. "I don't know him. And I barely know you."

"You fixed my dog once."

"I fix lots of dogs and wounded motherfuckers. Doesn't mean my gates open to everybody."

"I'm sorry. Is there anything I can offer you to help him? He's been bleeding all day. We've been on the road for hours. He's going to die."

"Maybe it's his time," Nola said.

The Professor stuck his hand out of the car window into the shrubs, waving a handful of postage stamps. His wound reopened and he bled out.

Nola kept a legitimate clinic. Uncluttered, considering the size of her home. By a window was a tall shelf crammed with medical textbooks, literature, fantasy, myth, and science fiction books. Images of Asclepius were common among the south-western ephemera on the walls and shelves. Also, voodoo fetishes and the art of Gustave Dore. Caged pets in every corner. A bouncy chinchilla. Floor to ceiling aquariums of tarantulas, snakes, iguanas and geckos. Cats walked around quietly. Five of them. One tuxedo, one black, three Russian Blues.

Photos of Sergeant Nola Jordana Aguilar and her platoon of brave women wearing desert camouflage. Huddled together in a dusty war zone in some desert hellhole. Framed medals, and rank insignias, certificates, plaques, awards. A shrine to the fallen, set upon an upside-down American flag.

When The Professor opened his eyes, he searched the low-lit room, feeling displaced and anxious. He felt himself floating above the table where he laid. At the far end of the room Nola stood in front of a mirror redressing a wound under her left arm, just above her ribcage. Her forearm was bandaged too. Post-burn scars snaked up her leg, shoulder, and neck. But those were from the war.

He caught his own reflection, and her eyes drilling back at him. He shook his head and adjusted his glasses: there were snakes slithering at her feet.

"Danielle?" He said, feeling heavy and immovable.

"She ain't here." Nola said. "Left yesterday."

"Where?"

"Fuck I know?"

"She said she was just going to keep driving."

"Then why'd you ask?"

"Sorry. Thank you for helping me. I'd be dead otherwise."

"I plucked it out, stitched you up." Nola said. "Gave you penicillin. By American medical standards you owe me seven million motherfucking dollars. We traded though. You ain't gonna miss them acid stamps, are you? White kids love buying anything I pass off as a narcotic. I could sell them green toothpaste on a cupcake and they'd buy it if they thought it was full of weed. I let you sleep as long as you needed. I'd just as soon take you out back to the grave I dug up but you're a scientist so you get a pass."

"Yes. *Scientist*." He said. "Thank you for sparing me the dirt nap."

"Whatever, motherfucker."

"I'm sure the acid will make a lot of local kids better adjusted than the crank they're smoking. Can I at least get my briefcase back?"

"It's empty. I don't care. When you're able to stand up you're going to help me out back."

"Okay."

"It's a big grave. Don't worry. The hole's already dug. Just need help moving shit into it."

"You dug my grave?"

"I said I spared you, didn't I?"

"You did. Are you here by yourself?"

"Motherfucker, you don't see my companions?"

Her menagerie stirred in their cages and aquariums.

"Sure, I do. Sorry." He said.

"And stop apologizing so much, you little bitch. Now, when the morphine wears off it's going to sting a little. When you can move your feet, get up and walk around outside."

"Our wounds are similar, coincidentally," he said. "But I don't want to open mine up and fuck up your good stitch work. I'm afraid to ask what happened to you."

Nola stared at him and his side began to hurt. She said,

"We just have to drag them inside the hole."

"*Them?* The grave?"

"Guess you were out when we brought you in. I've been at this for several days now and I don't like my momentum broken. I gotta finish it. Gives me a sense of completion. Ya dig?"

He searched the room again. Clarity came in slow waves. He glanced the medical certificates, medals, ribbons from the U.S. Marine Corps.

"So, you practice animal medicine mostly?" He said.

"Keeps my taxes legit."

"We are all participating in some major sins this week. We are conducting the dark business of the universe."

She stared at him for a long while before returning to her wound.

For the first time in days he could shut his eyes and not pass out. Every time he opened them it felt like a clean start. He stopped asking about his briefcase. He began to toy with a name change, new face, new town.

Then he was outside with her. It was a placid, late spring afternoon with the sun beaming through the trees. Turkeys and chickens fluttered by. He noticed bloody footsteps from the parked van to the house and back. How they formed a heart shape in the grass. He noticed a big lump of dirt where she'd dug a grave. And dried blood. Everywhere.

"This is one peaceful kingdom you have." The Professor said. "Despite the carnage."

Sitting in front of the fancy conversion van was a very dead man. He had gaping wounds like someone had a gunfight inside him, blasting their way out. Slumped and bent awkwardly in the grass, his chin rested on a wreath of gold jewelry. He wore a matching red and white leather sweat suit that reminded The Professor of a cereal box.

"Help me carry this nigga to the hole." Nola wore black overalls and combat boots. Together they dragged Demetrius a few feet to the trench. Looking down in it was the first time The Professor had seen a man disassembled where he no longer appeared to be a man. Just pieces of a man. Pieces of Boots. An arm here, torso there, a severed head. The Professor gagged and vomited but all that came out was foamy water.

"I'm burying this stupid nigga just as he is." Nola said. "Tacky-ass bootleg leather suit and all. Fuck his fake-ass Yeezys. We gone take his chains tho'. Them shits are real and worth a lot. Go ahead and start taking off his jewelry."

The Professor struggled around the bloody neck.

"Just yank them off, muthafucka!" Nola said. "It's all gonna get melted down anyway."

Cats played on the fence, and in the bushes. Some observed them from the back porch. One was peeing under a rosemary shrub. The Professor saw small headstones where deceased pets had been buried.

"How long were you in the Corps?" he said.

She didn't answer.

"A close friend of mine was a Marine," he said. "Served in Vietnam. Drank himself to death. *Semper fi.*"

The chains were off, so they rolled Demetrius on top of Boots. His body humped several inches above the hole. Boots, even in pieces, had taken up a lot of space.

"Shit," Nola said. "I didn't have a lot of time to do this. Didn't figure on this bear-sized muthafucka taking up so much room."

The stiches in her forearm opened and blood ran down her wrist. She clenched her arm, hunched over in pain. Grunting. Cursing and spitting. But the look in her eyes assured him she wasn't spent.

"I'm all fucked up and you've got stitches," she said. Her knuckles and fists were raw and bruised. "Let me reconfigure this shit. Reassemble this fucking puzzle."

"You got pigs?" He said. "You can feed dead bodies to pigs."

"I used to. I'd have to starve them for that, but I don't abuse my animals. Besides, these are some raunchy ass, roguish niggas, so, *no*. I wouldn't feed them to my worst enemies, and they *were* my worst enemies."

"You know what Orwell said, '*we do not merely destroy our enemies, we change them*'."

Her glare almost killed him.

"What about fire?" he said. "It gets everything going and clears out your karma."

Nola pressed her arm wound again, trying to heal it like her grandmother used to. She looked at him. Nodding. Agreeing. Grunting with each painful breath.

"Yeah, I thought about it," she said picking up a machete. She ran her thumb over the length of the blade. "But the neighbors. These crackers called the police the last time I burned leaves out of season. They definitely gonna know I'm roasting up some gangsta niggas. I was hoping not to have to chop another muthafucka up, but that's what we got going on right now."

"I'm starting to think you imagined her."

Phobos and Chuck carried on a conversation when silence allowed it.

"I saw her, man," Chuck said. "At the cemetery. While these clowns got fucked up on Sherm and you danced yourself to sleep, I went into the woods to piss and then I saw her. Black and beautiful. Glowing and vibrating. It was *her*."

"Were your glasses on? That area was kind of swampy. It was probably gas you saw. A vapor."

"There's no swamp there, man. I slapped myself retarded until my vision was clear. Who or what else could it be? She had a crown of thorns, a knife in her mouth, and snakes wrapped around her arms."

"And you didn't smoke any of that shit that turned them into zombies?"

"Nah, man. I've never messed with that shit. She was singing something. A melody I'd never heard. Said her name was, like, *Aranyani.* I have a suspicion she's with me, wherever I go. Like she's my protector. She was my nurse. She held my hand when I thought I was dying. Bathed me. Washed my balls."

"What kind of drugs did they have you on when you had your stroke?"

"It wasn't any drugs, man. Maybe I got too drunk or something. I don't even believe in ghosts."

"So, what about the girl you met at school? You said the same thing about her. You used to talk about her all the time."

"The one from MershTech? She was cute but she only used

to bring me lunch. She didn't save my life."

"Seems like that's always your story."

"Whatever, man," Chuck said. "I left school before finishing. Took a *different* career path."

"You gotta go to a real school."

"What are you talking about? It was a real school."

"MershTech is not affiliated. You can't transfer those credits, man."

"Who gives a shit? I graduated from the school of hard knocks. Why are we even talking about this? I lost the girl, but I kept the loan. Threw some parties. Paid off some strippers. Bought a house. Now I'm cleaning up messes. Doing passenger service. Making deliveries. It's all in my game plan, man."

Trash pushed his head between them. His breath smelled like urine had been used to put out a cigar factory fire.

"When the revolution comes," Trash said. "You won't have to worry about any of that. No loans, no paybacks. Houses for everybody. Free education and drugs for everybody. Free rent, free guns, and food for kittens."

"I don't think Communism works anymore, buddy," Phobos said. "If four people are getting paid and only two are doing the actual work, what's the fairness and equality in that? How's that benefit all?"

"Trust me, it works. It worked for Joe Stalin. It works for us. What we build will be ours. Our property, our food, our guns."

"Stalin was a murdering dictator."

"He was?" Chuck said.

Phobos nodded. "Research the Great Purge, dude."

"Are we there yet?" Ghoul Girl said.

"Amateurs," Trash said. "Keep steering. Don't let it pass you by. Don't find yourself up against the wall."

Phobos stiffened and sat up. He pointed a finger back at him. "Hold on. I know you. I fucking knew it when I smelled your cigarillo. You're *Jeff*!"

Chuck looked confused.

"Jeff Blink." Phobos said. "I remember you from Carbine Junior High. I remember you being in honors classes but you would hang out with the metal heads, smoking weed and getting dusted."

"Was it my monocle what gave me away?" Trash said. "Was it my youthful, revolutionary gleam? Don't say that you know me too loud because you have me mistaken with someone else."

"Of course, he has," Clown Face said. "Because the guy you mentioned used to hang out with grade school girls. He kidnapped two of them, and started a revolution. Graduated from a clown college."

"When it all reaches a climax," Ghoul Girl crept up on Phobos' left, chomping at his face. "He's going to end it in a gunfight with the cops, like *DeFreeze*. That is, if this 'Jeff' you speak of is even real."

The backseat trio knowingly grinned at each other. A cultish chortle passed between them. Ghoul Girl took it too far and cackled madly. The few who knew her well knew her jokes about throwing children into a woodchipper or setting fire to a wedding dress while the bride wore it were not really jokes. They were events.

Phobos searched for music on the radio. Ghoul Girl reached around him and shut it off.

"You gonna make a stink?" Trash placed the gun barrel at Phobos' head.

"No. I'm sick of all of your shit, though." Phobos said. "All of you!"

"Me too?" Chuck said.

"No, man. I can't wait 'til we fucking get there so I don't have to ever see their stupid faces again."

"We're gonna need a ride to Atlanta, boss." Trash said. "That was the deal."

"Goddamn it, no!"

"We'd love to drive ourselves back," Trash said. "But you saw what happened to our wheels. And we have a lot of love to spread around, if you know what I mean. We've been running for a while. This is nice. A Caddy. Next best thing to a limo."

"Great White," Chuck said.

"Running from where?" said Phobos.

"This campaign needed financing," Trash sucked his teeth. "We struggled, starved, and endured, so we were forced to commit some robberies."

"Struggled?" Phobos pressed his opened palms on the steering wheel. "Dude, you're a trust-fund punk! The fuck did you struggle about?"

Chuck said to Phobos, "Bank robbers, huh?"

"Weren't banks," Ghoul Girl said. "In any case there'd be more of us, but we lost some along the way."

Arguments droned. Not long after, in traffic as thick as mud, Phobos pounded the wheel with rage.

"Everybody shut the fuck up!" He shouted.

"Buddy, relax," Trash said. "Once we get to Koi's place, we're going to revolutionize how people get high. Rub out the competition."

"Is The Professor going to be there?" Clown Face said. "He's so smart." She was best when silent because she had the most childish and whiny voice of all of them.

"When we're done with Koi, we're taking this nationwide!" Trash sat back. "All the way, USA! *All the way, USA!*"

"All the way, USA!" The girls chanted.

"Koi is a good guy," Chuck said. "He's my friend."

"Yeah," Phobos said. "Can't let you do that. You guys are getting off the next exit."

The backseat trio went silent.

A fly buzzed on the dash.

Then Trash exploded. He shoved his gun at the back of Chuck's skull.

"I'll say when we're done, okay, you lousy bum!" Trash shouted. "I'm the one with all the firepower here. And the women. Stay focused. I'm not going to say it again. And you, keep fucking driving, asshole!"

"Don't fucking yell at me!" Phobos said. "It's my car! Get your fucking gun off his head! *Now!*"

"Dude," Chuck said. He elbowed him gently. "Everybody just relax. We can sort this out."

Trash held a bowie knife in his other hand against Phobos' neck.

"All right," Chuck said. He put his hands up. "You fucking win, Trash. Relax. Just relax."

"You fucking win, asshole." Phobos said. "You wanna flex the guns and power, do it. Get your thrills."

Trash mocked him. "It's not about you, bum boy. It's the movement. You're with us, or you're against us. The poet William Blake said, *'the road of excess leads to the balance of wisdom'*. Be wise. Keep driving. Keep quiet."

PART III: MADONNA OF FLIES

"She told us about the miracle but not the saint."

Gabriel Garcia Marquez

"Girl, you play too much," Demetrius said after getting another round of drinks.

The club was dark and dank. The dank was mad dank. Nola could only see him by the bling of his silver grill and gold chains. He danced around in his tacky leather sweat suit like the music was playing just for him.

"Thought you said you was gonna buy me dinner?" Nola said. She circled a finger around the rim of her cocktail glass.

"Who me?" Demetrius said. His sentences ended with unnecessary chuckling.

"I don't dig no cheap mothafuckas."

"I ain't cheap, girl." He flashed a cash roll from his jacket pocket.

"Nigga, is you high?" She said. "That ain't no knot. It's probably bigger than your dick though. And that ain't saying much."

"Girl, whatchoo know about dis dick? It's too early for me to unroll it right now."

"Uh huh." She sipped her drink and gazed from him to the bar. A gaze that told him, *there's plenty other niggas out chea that'll buy a girl dinner.*

"Baby girl." He went for her hand. Snake rings wrapped around her long fingers, over her knuckles and wrists.

Nola slapped his hand away.

"Nigga, I will stab you," she said. "Call me baby girl again."

"Why you playin'?" He said. "Aye, your profile said you was in the military. Whatchoo, a soldier? Whatchoo know about dat? Been to Iraq?"

"I ain't make that up."

"Word? You seen combat?"

"Nigga, yeah," she said. "Fuck you think a soldier do in Iraq?"

"So, you killed some *haji* niggas?"

"I was communications and medical."

"You fixed up shot-up niggas?"

"And blown up *niggas,* treated suicide *niggas*. Mothafuckas who shot their own toes just to get out of the war."

"Word? Yo, that's real."

"Course it is. As real as me."

"That's some traumatic shit. Must be hard for a woman to be out there like that."

"How's that? Nigga, it's hard being a woman in *here*. It's hard being a woman *anywhere*."

"Yeah, but you was in war, shit blowing up, and niggas dying around you."

"Wasn't any different than being a man out there. Gender don't matter, race don't matter. You bleed the same, you die the same when you're in a war."

The conversation was more duck-and-cover as the night progressed. Demetrius curled closer and closer around her, slowly closing the space between them. Nola's hand hovered over her drink to keep contaminants out. To keep *him* out of it. The music volume increased every fifteen minutes or so. Pink neon lights formed pulsating halos around them. Demetrius kept ordering more for drinks himself. Turquoise colored drinks with cherries on top.

Nola scanned the bar, looked at every face. She missed her reptile babies. And her furry babies. Better to be with them than these reptiles.

"Whatchoo got planned?" she said.

He chuckled behind his glass. "Whatchoo want?"

"Nigga, I'm bored. Whatchoo do for fun? I seen pictures of you shooting off guns and drinking yak with your boys. What do *you* do?"

"I could do you."

"Nah, homie. You can't. This ain't the place right now. You gotta grease the monkey if you wanna get funky."

He drove a maroon car with chrome trimming. It had tiny wheels with large chrome rims with a chassis so close to the ground that it sparked whenever it hit a bump. Or a pebble. The raised front end tended to. The interior smelled of marijuana and cherry air freshener.

"It's like a fucking porch swing up in here." She said. "Back and forth, back and forth..."

"Always got jokes," he said.

"What?"

"You heard me." He tilted back in his seat, driving with one hand, holding a joint in the other. He puffed and passed. "We can go back to my crib."

"You stay with your mom?" Nola said. The seat cradled her like a giant hand. She took a puff and passed it back.

"Haha. No. Fuck you think?"

"I think this blunt is busted. Imma let you taste some of mine."

"Uh huh. Bring it."

"Admit it: you ain't got nothing else going on tonight. What the fuck you do for fun?"

"What the fuck *you* do for fun?"

"Nigga, you asked me out."

"Aight. Imma show you."

"Better not whip out yo' dick."

"Nah, boo. I'll show you something."

He drove northwest on the highway two cities over, winding up in a degenerate neighborhood where boxed buildings and warehouses sat dark and abandoned.

"You wanna see a show?" he said.

"I'm down," she said. "What, your mom's twirling 'round the pole at Blue Flame tonight?"

"Bitch, nah. You got jokes about everything? Imma take you to where my cousin Boots runs things."

"Boots Tumbler is your cousin?"

"Yeah. First cousin. We inseparable. You hungry?"

"You finally buying me dinner?"

"What I'm trying to tell you is they got BBQ wings and ribs where we going."

Smoked food was the first thing she smelled when they finally made it to the warehouse. He drove down an alleyway to a lot paved with oyster shells and parked behind a pile of tires.

"Where's Boots?" she said, surveying the surrounding piles of garbage.

"He's inside," Demetrius said. "Dang girl. Why you all up on his nuts?"

"Just curious. He's legendary. I wanna get a picture with him."

They walked to the front entrance. He bought her a BBQ plate where the meat sat on top of white bread and hot pickles. The door guy handed out Playstations to the first couple of ticketholders. They entered the warehouse as dogs were being brought in. The darkness was suffocating until they reached the pit. Industrial lamps lit up the action and the multiple spectators.

The BBQ she ate was bloody, but it was the metallic air she was tasting. Slick with the sweat of men, mostly black, some Mexican, some white, and a few Asians. The few women there gawked at her. The look Nola returned pierced them deep in their souls, and the souls of their unborn children.

Dogs were pulled in by their keepers and lowered into the pit. Once the fights began, owners couldn't touch them. Rules allowed them to stand by the pit and yell, but touching would forfeit the fight. Fights tended to last twenty minutes to an hour. The shouting was deafening.

Nola stood beside Demetrius behind chicken wire and watched four fights. The crowd was savage and bloodthirsty. Fiery eyes and drooling maws. Fistfuls of sweaty currency. Boots rolled out and circled the arena giving out high-fives. He was still bandaged but mobile. Demetrius waved him down and they found a quiet place away from the pit to talk. Nola was introduced.

Boots parked in front of her, reviewing her. She was wearing a black T-shirt and maroon hot pants. Oxblood knee-high boots. Crimson wig. Her arm, shoulder and neck bore dermal scarring. Boots had a look of disgust when he saw the scars. He pressed his bandaged neck when he spoke.

"Damn, girl. Where you from?"

"From out my mom's pussy." Nola said.

Demetrius laughed so hard he folded over.

"Nigga," Boots said. "Better get your girl."

"I ain't his girl." Nola said.

"Come on girl, where you from?"

"Atlanta."

"All right now. I'm down with the A-T-L. That's my birthplace. You ever seen shit like this before?"

"Not really." She swallowed hard. "When is it over?"

"We here all night, fam." Boots said.

"I'd rather be at a casino or the track."

"Play them horses?"

"Horses, dogs. I don't care."

Demetrius said, "Yo, we can leave after this." He curled around her again. This time she let him put his arm around her waist.

"Come on, girl." Boots said. "There's money to be made right here. Put some down."

"Too noisy up in here." She said.

They went back and watched another fight.

"Greatest animal ever lived," Boots said, clapping. He collected money and went outside to get BBQ. Demetrius and Nola followed.

"Where's ya bar at?" She said. "I need a drink."

"Let's go." Demetrius had his arm around her. She allowed his embrace, as they stood by the entrance. More people had lined up waiting to get in.

"I think you had enough, girl." Demetrius said.

Boots was saluting and shouting out to people that came and went. He tore into half a blackened chicken from the BBQ stand.

"You staying for the next round?" Boots asked her.

"I've seen enough," Nola said. "You boys just gonna stay here all night?"

"I don't know. Depends."

"I'm not too far from here if you're down to take the party elsewhere."

Boots looked up at Demetrius. Demetrius smiled, pulled her closer and kissed her.

Getting situated behind the wheel of his conversion van took a long time. Boots first had to lower the access lift on the left side of the van, then roll himself on it. Then strap himself in. Lift himself up. Secure the chair. Unstrap. Jump into the captain's chair. Rotate and adjust himself behind the steering wheel. Strap on the prosthetic calves to the pedals. Make sure the wheelchair was secured behind his seat.

Nola sat behind Demetrius. The interior smelled like old marijuana, but the air freshener smelled like pink lemonade and it irritated her nose. Demetrius blasted the radio and they went. As the traveling discotheque rolled, a small mirror ball spun a galaxy of lights inside the van. Beside the wheelchair was a small footlocker and a car battery with jumper cables. There was a dog cage behind her.

"We had some *good* dogs tonight, *boyyyy*." Boots said. "I ain't done. We goin' back later."

"Most def, cuz." Demetrius said.

They had to shout to hear each other.

"How many animals die there each time?" Nola said.

"Depends," Boots said. "It's surprising how those owners love they dogs and don't want to see them go down. It be killing them when it happens and they dog loses. And sometimes, dogs don't die. But they was all good dogs tonight!"

"What about the bad dogs?"

"Ain't no bad dogs. If they give all and can't do it no more, they get put out."

"They get shot or get a shot that put them to sleep." Demetrius said. "Or sometimes they get those wires there put to them. *Bzzzzt.*"

The twirl of disco lights obscured her rolling tears of rage.

"Where do you ditch them afterwards?" She said.

"We used to burn them but almost got caught," said Demetrius.

"White people love to call the cops on niggas when they make fire," Boots said. "We've changed the pit location multiple times. Plus, we burned down one of the warehouses that time we set the dogs on fire. Now I have my boy Chuck haul them off."

"Chuck Farley?" Nola said.

"Yeah, that's my boy. He crazy. How you know him?"

"He was one of my patients when I was a nurse. Goofy Chuck."

"You fuck him?" Demetrius said.

"Did I fuck you?"

"Not yet."

"Keep wishing, muthafucka."

"For real, though," Boots said. "You know Chuck?"

"Yeah. I just said he was my patient. Make sure you treat him right. He's a good man."

"He good, but he owes me money, 'cause he fucked up. I guess he ain't tell you what he did?"

"I never heard him talk about you."

They stopped at a red light. Boots looked at her, stared at her thighs. Behind the stream of mirror light Boots saw fire in her eyes. He felt a momentary chill. The road was so dark the van seemed to be floating through space.

"Anyway," Boots said. "That's between me and Chuck. He

doing some side work for me. He gonna catch up and pay me back."

"Don't hurt my Chuck," she said.

They found a package store, stopped and stocked up. Boots went through the procedure of dismounting and rolling out. He didn't trust that Demetrius knew what brand of sweet blunts he liked best. Or that the malt liquor had to have the right kind of chill to it. Nola found his movement in and out to be more tedious than before but while they were both inside the store, she rummaged through the footlocker. She found old tapes and CD's of Boots' failed rap group, *Tum-Bla*. On the cover it was him and his crew wearing leather sweat suits, back when Boots had legs. She found bags of weed portioned into small sellable baggies and took as many as she could fit into her purse. Loaded syringes, capsules, vials of tranquilizers that she also smuggled in her purse. In fact, she put the bags of weed back to make room for them. There were miles of audio cables, flyers to last year's New Year's Eve Smash Bash, but nothing else of value. When they came out of the store, she straightened up.

The lift for the wheelchair whined for a good while until Boots was back on board and climbing into his seat. Demetrius carried an armful of liquor and snacks.

"You good? Let's go." Boots said. He started up the van and the music blasted. The throbbing mobile discotheque took off into the night.

"Damn, dis some country ass roads." Demetrius said, chewing on a Slim Jim. "Look like they hung a brotha or two out here."

"When in Rome," said Nola.

After several miles, the van curved off the road into a dark entryway. Trees and shrubs covered the van until it could barely fit the driveway. Boots stopped at the gate. The radio went silent. The head beams sent animal silhouettes dancing against the trees.

"Whatchoo got, peacocks and shit?" Demetrius said. He didn't chuckle that time. He looked spooked.

"Turkeys," Nola said.

"It's tight getting out on this side." Demetrius pushed the door hard against shrubbery.

Boots looked at her. "I'm trapped on my side too. You gonna open up this gate, baby girl? Let's eat them turkeys."

"Eat pig shit." She'd hid a syringe in her palm, with her thumb on the plunger.

He grabbed her wrist.

"Look, baby girl. We goin' in. Drink some yak and smoke some shit. Either you gonna fuck or we're gonna fuck. Got that? Either way you fuckin'."

"Think so, muthafucka?" She tilted her head and twinkled her eyes in the sweetest way possible. Then she raised the syringe with her free hand. He looked at it oddly.

"Oh, so you a murk—"

She stabbed it into his eye and pushed the plunger. He released her, screaming and crying, swatting his face like it was covered in bees. The tranquilizer took immediate effect. He choked and slumped.

"Girl, you outcho gotdamn mind!" Demetrius reached for the gun in his armpit. Nola pinned him to the seat with a bear hug, hooked her right arm around his neck and choked him. Her other hand went up into his jacket and found his gun. She pressed the barrel into his rib cage and squeezed every shot she could. A bullet shattered his collar bone, two exited from his right side into the door, and another burst through his chest plate, wounding her forearm. Then he was very still and dead.

Boots jolted, waving a gun around, shooting wildly. Bullets ripped into Demetrius. Nola balled up in her seat, taking hits to her left side. A bullet burned close to her ribs. Shrieking, she grabbed the gun from Boots, shooting him twice in his stomach. To let him bleed out. He howled louder than she did. She punched his face and he was out in a sea of stars.

She wanted him alive.

"Wake up, nigga."

Nola had rotated his seat so that he faced her. He was strapped in tightly. She punched him awake.

"I had to make sure it was you. Didn't wanna kill the wrong mothafucka."

She slowly pulled the syringe from his eye. The socket looked like a bleeding mouth. His eyeball had deflated. His face was swollen like rotten fruit, head bouncing on a rubbery neck. She beat his face repeatedly with slow, well-aimed blows until she was satisfied. Until her knuckles bled. In between punches she held her punctured side.

She'd opened the front gate and driven the van inside her yard by pushing the seat back and sitting on his lap. She'd parked it next to the crumbling mobile home with the tree growing out of it. Once upon a time her mother had lived in there.

"Smell like shit up in here," Nola said and lit an ashtray full of weed. "You out? You awake? Where are you right now, muthafucka? You at the *threshold*?"

She decked him again and his head snapped sideways. She nearly fell over from her aching wounds. Felt like one of her ribs had cracked.

"You shouldn't be feeling a thing, as much as I pumped into you. I mean, you might. I don't give a fuck either way. Had to make sure it was you, Boots. Boots Tumbler. Local narcotics entrepreneur, loan shark, animal abuser, *'rapper.'* By the way, I bought your tape and it was garbage. Straight trash."

"Grrl you crayyzzee." He could barely assemble a sentence.

"You right. You right, dawg. In fact, that's why you're here. *Dawg*. Before you shit yourself again, I'm going to pay my buddy Chuck's debt to you. Get him in the clear, the poor boy. And then you're going to pay back mine. After this, you won't ask anymore of Chuck. Ever. You won't bleed another dime from him. Truthfully though, you're never going to see Chuck ever again. You owe him your life and your freedom. When he burned his house, he did you a favor because they was coming for you. I bet you didn't know that, muthafucka.

"But besides all that, *you took my dog*. Chuck told me he recognized my dog when he was cleaning up after one of your fights. I'd told him he'd gone missing, taken from the storefront where I usually left him tied up. That's my bad. I'd sent him a picture of him one night when we'd been talking. Chuck wanted nudes but instead I sent him a picture of Agee, short for *Agamemnon*. Ain't that some coincidental shit? You stole my dog, and because of you, my dog is dead. *Massacred*."

"It werreent me," Boots mumbled through a broken jaw. *"The fight killed him. Shoulda been a better fighter."*

"You know, he wasn't even a fighting dog? You took him because he'd never been around that, and you wanted to show a dog getting ripped up for those bloodthirsty muthafuckas. You knew he didn't stand a chance. You knew he'd get chewed up if you threw him in the pit. You knew that's what the crowd was thirsty for. I hope I find every muthafucka that bet on those dogs. You know what I'm going to do? I'm going to free those caged dogs, then I'm going to lock those people in that warehouse and torch it. I'm gonna sit outside and watch it burn just so I can hear their screams."

Boots grunted and vomited. The smell made her wince.

"Are you done now?" Nola yelled into his face. "I really hate going into this ugliness, but there is something sinister instilled in me. It's been there ever since I was a little girl, defending myself with a stick in the Honduran country side. Something sinister that goes back in my family history. And that's what's going to make this really ugly."

She rotated the chair so he faced the steering wheel. She stood behind him and grabbed his forehead, sticking a combat knife deep into the left side of his head, just between his ear and jawline. As deep as it could go. Then she swept it under and across with one slick move. Tongue and gristle exploded through his neck.

"In combat training we learned to kill by slitting the necks of innocent goats. I mean, if you can't kill an animal how you gonna kill a combatant? I only had to do it once to know what it took, and what it would feel and look like. Then I got more practice with all the *haji's* that I slaughtered in combat in that sandnigger desert. How did you get over the smell of dead dogs? I never did. The smell of carnage. The heat coming off the blood. Steaming guts. Let me tell ya, a commendation medal don't heal shit."

She only had to make the fatal motion once. She wiped her blade and tucked the knife back in her boot where she'd carried it. His chest stopped heaving. His body settled. She experienced meditative peace in watching him die. An hour passed. She watched him until he was petrified. An effigy of blood and sweat.

The next morning Nola stood on her back porch wearing only underwear and bandages, drinking a cup of coffee. When she finished, she walked down to the mound of dirt she'd dug up. She ground her feet into the soil while stretching her arms, open palms kissed by sunrays. She inhaled.

Flies swarmed her. She dropped to her knees in prayer, then speared her arms into the black soil, soil darker than her. Digging. *Diving.* Feeling the cool earth sooth her hands and arms. Her face, torso, and legs. She pressed into the dirt and buried herself, inhaling the musk, swimming in soil. Taking in mouthfuls of black earth, letting it fill her ears and nostrils. She rolled over and faced the sky. A blanket of flies smothered her, buzzing over her bruised knuckles and fingers, in her hair, over her nipples and into her belly button. She opened her mouth. They crawled over her lips and ran across her teeth.

She was completely buried when she lifted from the grave, gnashing and clawing her way to the surface. She went inside the house and returned with two machetes. They'd belonged to her grandmother in Honduras.

Covered in dirt she opened the driver door, oblivious to the smell or flies. She cut the seatbelt and Boots plopped on the dirt like wet garbage. The flies followed. He looked like an old leather loveseat someone had left out in the rain. She began dismantling, chopping like her grandmother did sugarcane. Demetrius' body sat against the front of the van, occasionally burping. She'd forgotten about him but wondered how a bullet-riddled body could still be gassy. She spit at him.

It was sloppy work. She'd emptied Boots' pockets of cash and drugs, his guns, and jewelry. He had to be disrobed to make it easier for her to sever his joints and sockets.

Arms first. At the elbows. Then chop the shoulders. She'd already gotten a head start on the decapitation. When she finished dismantling him, she felt dizzy and dehydrated. She didn't have the strength to bury Demetrius.

She went into the house and showered, contemplating how to get rid of the van. A few hours later she had uninvited guests driving up to her gate.

Knock-knock.

"Who's there?"

"The Plumber."

"The shitter's fine. We don't need a plumber."

When they opened the door there was a man in a short coat holding a carpetbag.

"Haha! Are you a stripper? Hey, did someone order an old-dad stripper?"

"Are we gonna drive through Blade Runner City?" Trash asked with a most childish and annoying tone. Clown Face was bursting with the same glee. Personalities blurred, became fuzzy, cross-faded into each other. Difficult to discern who was whom, and who spoke for whom. They passed around their guns, their makeup, a formaldehyde-soaked blunt.

"That's the long way to Koi's place," Phobos said. He'd escaped for a while, day-dreamed most of the last hour away, and now was rudely yanked back. "And I want to get there soon. I was going to take Service Road 73."

"Stay the course," Trash said. "Stop when I tell you. In fact, don't stop. Run all the lights. You'll know when we're there. There'll be a parade with sparklers, fireworks, and all that rhythm. We'll have us a good, old fashion zombie stomp."

Ghoul Girl clapped.

"Go on," Trash said. "We're gonna line them all up against the wall and get 'em lit. If the formula works, they'll turn on each other and just like that, the competition is gone. And then, guess who's on top?"

Phobos glanced at Chuck.

"Ever heard of Boots Tumbler?" Chuck said.

"Boots?" Trash said. "Yeah, I know Boots."

"I don't think he'll approve."

"That's why we have guns."

"But he has guns. And goons."

Trash stopped. Ghoul Girl put the joint back in his mouth, and he sucked on it hard.

"Look," Trash said and fogged the car. "Shut the fuck up,

okay?"

Several police cars passed them, speeding towards an accident. An ambulance followed.

Chuck tightened up in his seat. *"Dude."*

"Don't worry about it." Phobos said.

"Everybody, just cool it," Trash said. "Don't shit yourselves. The world is anarchy. What would the cops want with us? Phobos, you know this, you rebel. Get by however you can. Authorities be damned. We'll police ourselves. After the party we'll recruit whoever's left standing. Build our ranks up again. You two, you're grandfathered in."

"Gee, thanks," Chuck said. "But I have a cat to take care of."

"Who's feeding her?" Phobos said.

"I left her a big bowl full of food. But I know she misses me. And I miss her."

Everyone rubbernecked the accident when they passed it. Traffic funneled four lanes into two.

The Great White took the loop that curled around Blade Runner City with its miles of billboards and chrome castles. The metropolis had a futurist design like those 1970s science fiction book covers. And just on the other side, to the east, was the shore. The Atlantic. The Great White drove straight toward the drop-edge span to nowhere.

"I'm feeling a little depressed," Chuck said.

"Thought you loved the beach," Phobos said.

Chuck shrugged. "It's all right. These places are all starting to look the same."

"But look at that water. You'll think you're dreaming it. I'm seriously considering Mexico."

"I feel you." Chuck yawned and stretched and farted. "We almost there? I gotta shit."

"Move to San Francisco," Trash said. "They let all the bums shit on the street there."

There was a tight, unbearable silence the closer they got to West River. Then Chuck's phone rang. Phobos looked in the rearview at the passengers. Chuck looked back there too. The ringtone was an 8-bit version of The Misfits song "Last Caress".

"Can I answer it?" Chuck said.

"Can you?" Trash said. Midday sunlight reflected off the buildings, lighting up his face. "I fucking love that song. But answer it already."

Chuck flipped his phone open. "Hello?"

"Hey," Freebird said. "Is this you?"

"Who else would it be?" Chuck said.

"It ain't your mom."

Chuck mouthed who it was to Phobos.

"Where are you?" Chuck said.

"You'd never guess." Freebird said loud enough that the whole car could hear it.

"In jail?"

"Haha. Fuck you. I'm near a beach. I'm eating tacos. Where the fuck you think?"

"Mexico? How?"

"No fucking way," Phobos said.

"No fucking way, dude," Chuck said. "You'd have to have flown there. And what about the truck? The load?"

"Ask your mom," Freebird said. He laughed a good ten seconds with that one.

"Fuck you, man!" said Chuck. "Did you ditch it? Where's the truck?"

"Relax." Freebird laughed. "Wait. Is this your burner?"

"Always."

"Anyway, I took a detour. Stopped in New Orleans and found some friends that helped me out. Then I took a plane down to Mexico. I said fuck it. I'm on vacation, boys. You sound a little uptight there, buddy. I have a plan to bring you guys down here. The sooner, the better. Listen to this."

"But what about the load?" Chuck said.

"Don't worry about that. I'm happy to report that in the war between reality and me getting some sun, reality is losing. Honestly, I've been at the beach since I got here. How are you guys doing?"

"Not so hot, man. Still on the road."

"You should be at the beach already, knee-deep in it."

"We're not."

"Sure, buddy." Freebird said. "I understand. But hear me out: I got the best job lined up for you guys. Get this: I met a guy who owns a cemetery in San Fernando. Business is fucking booming. Caskets are selling like tacos! You know what I mean? You'll be doing what you do there, but you'll do it here."

"Why would I go there to do it?"

"Uh, near the beach? Get paid per body in American dollars? You'll live like a king, plus digging graves builds muscle. Maybe you can get one of those doctors here to fix your leg. I got it all mapped out for you two. Come down and *dig brother, dig!* I'll call you guys later. Like, later-later." Freebird disconnected.

A crescent moon appeared early that afternoon. The sky was a profound blue, rimmed with orange clouds. El Alacran arrived through the back fence. It is unknown if he climbed it, jumped it, or went through it. Most likely he unlatched the back gate, closing it behind him as he drifted in. He walked around the pool and slipped in via the kitchen door. The party had hit a pitch and nobody noticed him. The house had been steaming for days. He looped in and out of each room, surveying, *sniffing*. Floating through clouds of narcotic smog. A smoke machine pumped out thick clouds on which a movie was being projected. Pulsing disco lights covered the cloudy ceiling. Music vibrated the floor and walls. Every room had its own musical theme. Hip-hop here, sludge-rock there, jazz piping out of the bathroom. Occasionally the smoke machine would hiss, and he'd hear giggling.

He didn't much walk as float through the maze of the house. Every room lit a different color scheme. A different scent to every room, not all of them pleasant. Bodies on the floor, bodies on tables, on couches, and seats. Bodies dancing. He studied their profiles, walking through them as if they were ghosts. Memorized faces, clothing styles. Shoes, jewelry, watches, and phones. The people they were speaking to or seen with. All dedicated to memory.

El Alacran wasn't using poison today. Too many peripherals. They'd have to send another team to clean up after him and that would result in a deduction out of his pocket. But they could at least blame it on the communal punch bowl.

After scanning every single face, he saw him, through the smoke and strobe lights. Working the DJ table. The one with the thick glasses and flipped up ball cap, stirring platters on the turntable. Sipping from a bottle of Everclear he kept by his equipment.

The DJ was accosted by random revelers giving him money for the little tiny bags he handed back. Calling out songs, cheering him.

"Bobby DJ!"

Koi Pond stood beside him pretending to know how to program the music.

"Hey, you know that guy, Boots?" Bobby DJ, *aka Damien Dust, aka Damon Fucks*, said. His voice was low and nasally.

Koi rolled his eyes. Then he started dancing.

"I don't think he likes me." Bobby DJ said.

"He's gonna have to face up to the competition," Koi said. "He wants to draft The Professor, but he's mine. Boots can stay in the A. Yeah, I accepted his coke bomb. Don't mean I'm gonna suck his dick."

Koi dipped when he heard *knock-knock* at the door.

El Alacran slithered behind the mixing table. Before Bobby DJ could object, El Alacran noticed the one called Koi Pond open the front door. He was able to get a good glimpse of The Plumber standing at the threshold, very business-like but wielding his tool. And then he went to work. No one noticed the DJ collapse with a broken neck. No one had seen when The Plumber crushed Koi Pond's skull with a monkey wrench, leaving him dead at the door.

El Alacran waited within the flatulent fog until it was time to move.

Wasn't long before a wave of panic set in and chaos took over. Like dominoes, one triggered the other, pushed the other who pushed the other, pouring out of the house. For a moment the assassins saw each other, nodding mutual admiration. The Plumber waited in the smog. El Alacran vanished. Both still creeping within the house.

Phobos circled the neighborhood, lost.

"I can't remember which house it is," he said.

"Hey boss," Chuck told Trash. "Thought you said there'd be a parade welcoming you."

"It would suck terribly to have to kill you right now." Trash put his gun to Chuck's head. "But I have to save my ammo."

Phobos listened for the sound of throbbing beats. He looped back again and there it was, a psychedelic oasis in suburbia. Three cars in the driveway, four on the street, two at the front of the neighboring house. There was a gap between the driveway and the gravel lawn. Just enough for the Great White to fit.

"Keep the motor hot," Trash said. "Company: present *Sherm!*"

The armed trio jumped out like clown commandos, creeping low. Ghoul Girl stood in front of the Great White holding her machine gun and smoking a cigarette. Trash and Clown Face went to the front entry and knocked. And knocked.

Music thudded behind the door. *Ootz ootz ootz.*

"Dude, we gotta send a signal inside," Chuck said. "What kind of stupid plan is this?"

"About as stupid as driving dead bodies to Mexico." Phobos pulled the headband over his eyes and shook his head.

"Come on, man. I can't just sit here. What's Koi's number?"

"I never call him. Isn't it programmed in your phone?"

"It's a burner. No."

The front door busted open and a torrent of revelers came out screaming.

"Hi everybody," Trash said offering a fresh blunt in one hand. *"We're with the Church of Slipknot! and Hello Kitty, and we'd like for you—"*

The panicked horde plowed over them. Clown Face got trampled and her machine gun got kicked out of her hand. When she reached for it, her arm and hand were crushed under a freight train of naked bodies.

"It's a raid!"

"The Second Coming!"

"Bobby DJ didn't even play my request!"

"Koi's dead!"

Information Society's "What's On Your Mind (Pure Energy)" played somewhere in the house. Trash took a stance like the commandos he'd watched in training videos. He dodged people, inching closer to the front door. No takers on the *Sherm*.

From the threshold he looked inside. Koi Pond lay dead at his feet. The house emptied. People were exiting out of windows and side doors and out the back. He looked back at Clown Face. She looked rough, laid out and trampled. He watched her twitch and he smiled. He looked at Ghoul Girl. She waved at him. He went to go back inside the house and a monkey wrench came flying into his face, laying him out cold. The Plumber appeared out of the pot smog, slowly walking outside. He bent over and picked up the monkey wrench lodged in Trash's face. The Pope of Irony never had a pretty face begin with. Beautiful eyes though. No shame in crushing that idiot skull of his.

The Plumber had the authority to make executive decisions in the field. Would be a shame to just bash in the face of this woman in clown makeup but that's precisely what he did. A doublehanded blow with the monkey wrench crushed her skull. He didn't want the poor girl in a coma for the rest of her stupid life. The family would have to settle for a closed casket.

Gunfire sputtered the driveway. The machine gun spray pierced his shoulder and ear. It was so unexpected that he hated himself for it. He'd spend the next few days castigating himself for it.

Ghoul Girl stood on the hood of the Great White, shooting. The Plumber flung a monkey wrench at her, but she took cover beside the car.

The rest of his tools were still in his carpetbag inside the house. He reached for Trash's machine gun. As it was standard procedure to adapt however necessary in the field, he aimed and fired.

Suddenly the Great White roared to life and rolled forward, destroying a small garden at the front of the house. Then it pulled back, smashing the fender of a parked car before speeding off down the street leaving Ghoul Girl exposed. Several rounds sprayed her side and chest. At The Plumber's feet, Trash flinched and farted. The Plumber looked down and emptied the clip, and then threw the machine gun aside. He straightened his coat and walked back into the house leaving a trail of blood. He walked past El Alacran, grabbed his carpetbag, and disappeared off the property, around the pool, over the fence.

El Alacran walked out the front door, carrying the bottle of Evercler he'd snatched from the DJ's table. He found Ghoul

Girl shivering, pocked with bullet holes. Her makeup was melting. He stood over her, spraying a mouthful of liquor at her.

"I don't usually break character," he said in English. His voice was pleasantly soft. "But this is for my family. Whatever demon possessed you to jealousy and their destruction, you owe them." He lit a pack of matches and set her aflame. He backed away but not so he couldn't smell her char or enjoy her screams.

Phobos and Chuck watched Ghoul Girl get mowed down. Her eyes had stayed with them, pleading until their brightness was snuffed. Phobos yanked the car into the street and drove. From the rearview they saw a flash of fire and could hear screams.

"Phobos." Chuck said.

The Great White pushed 85MPH.

"Yeah?" said Phobos.

"We gotta go back home. *Now*. I shit myself."

"Aw, dude"

"I got shot."

Phobos noticed the cracked window and small holes. And blood on the passenger door.

There was a vacuum in the car now that it was just the two of them. Even with a bullet wound Chuck felt a sense of relief, sweet as a mother's hug. He laid in the back seat, holding his arm, covered in blood.

"You're going to make it buddy," Phobos said.

The Great White pushed 90MPH.

"I wanna say it's a flesh wound but they're all flesh wounds, goddamn it." Chuck said. "The bullet is in there and I fucking feel it. Close to the bone. Goddamn it hurts. Also, one of those dumbasses stuck gum on the seat back. *What the?* There's half a human skull back here, man! And one of those goth chicks left their panties on the floor. *Gross.*"

"Fuck. I'm tired," Phobos said. "I'm so tired. We're low on gas and we have a long way to go. Call Freebird."

Chuck flipped open his phone and dialed.

"He's not answering."

He tried a few more times.

"What the fuck just happened?" Phobos shook his head.

"Probably the universe delivering comeuppance on everything and everyone all at once. Including us."

"Still doesn't tell me what really happened. Were they waiting on the clowns to show up? Did that man really kill them with a monkey wrench?"

When they crossed into the next town, they parked behind a gas station. Phobos bandaged Chuck with whatever he could find. He cleaned the wound with water, wiping it down with bathroom paper towels. Wrapped it the best he could with paper towels and electrical tape found under the seats.

"Shit happens," Phobos said. "I really don't want to go back to Atlanta now."

"Me neither." Chuck looked dead but was coherent. He rested his head, breathing through his mouth. "Boots will be waiting. He's gonna be pissed."

Chuck's phone rang. He scrambled to answer it.

"Is it Freebird?" Phobos said.

Chuck flipped it open and his face calmed. He blushed. After a brief conversation he closed it.

"She lives in Rome." He said. "You'll finally get to meet her."

"That's 200 miles away. Do you think you might bleed out and die before we get there?"

"Not planning on it. I've never been shot before, so I don't know. But dude, that was her. She called *me*. Said she'll take this out of me and sew me up. For a favor."

"There's always something."

"I told you she was my guardian angel. Change of plans."

"Dude, that's far to go when you're bleeding to death."

"I'm not dying. I promise."

"She just wants to be friends," Chuck said. "And I'm okay with that. Maybe I'll just hold her hand. If she lets me."

"I don't believe in faerie tales or angels," Phobos said.

"She'll bring me back to life."

They sped toward Rome. Gassed up, scared, sweating and bleeding. Speedometer, gas pedal, road. Repeat.

Freebird called. Chuck flipped his phone open.

"Where've you been?" Chuck said. "Been trying to reach you all afternoon."

"Dude, I'm on the beach," Freebird said.

"Bad news, man." Chuck said.

"Uh oh. Put me on speaker. Who else is there?"

"Just Phobos."

"So, you delivered the passengers?"

"Yeah, but things got complicated."

"Well, whatever. That's all I need to hear. I don't have time for complications right now. I want you guys to really consider what I'm offering."

"What's that?" Phobos said.

Chuck was fading in and out.

"Stay with me, buddy." Phobos said.

Chuck gave him a weak thumbs-up from the backseat.

"Fuck all else you have going on right now," Freebird said. "Because I want you guys down here *pronto!* Or at least in time for Christmas. Words don't do justice to this place. There's amazing food and pretty brown girls. And Spanish isn't that hard to learn. *Buenos dias! Donde esta la tequila?* You'll love it here."

"We can't go now," Phobos said. "Chuck's been shot!"

"Shot? Buddy, what happened? What the fuck? Come down and let these doctors look at you."

"You just got there," Phobos said. "It's a little soon for a hard sell."

"I'm bleeding out, man!" Chuck said.

"They've got miracle doctors here," Freebird said. "You can get any type of drug you want!"

Chuck groaned. "I can't go to Mexico if I'm dead, asshole!"

"How much more do you owe Boots?"

"Like acres worth of *trees*. I think he's sent some guys after us."

"Well, wouldn't it make sense for y'all to come down here? They can't hurt you if they can't find you. Did Chuck tell you about the work I have lined up? That is, if you don't mind digging graves in the desert."

"How's that?" Phobos said.

"There's a demand like a motherfucker for that kind of labor. Unless you wanna be a drug mule. Or coyote. I got those connections too."

"Hard pass," said Chuck.

"I'll dig some graves," Phobos said.

"That's the enthusiasm I like to hear," said Freebird. "Of course, that's all entry-level shit, but there's always room to grow. Tell him about the benefits, Chuck. I mean, if you guys wanna stay trash pandas in Atlanta, be my guest."

"Listen, dude," Chuck said. "I'm going to spend the rest of the night getting a bullet taken out of me."

"What?"

"For real, dude. If I die, I'll let you know."

Nola had the gate opened for them by the time the Great White arrived. A man with glasses and a trench coat waved them in. Nola and the man were both covered in dirt and blood. The man had a weird smile, and Phobos thought he recognized him.

Chuck slept. He was filthy. They removed him quickly from the backseat and brought him to the clinic without saying much to each other.

"I'm sorry I missed the party," The Professor said, opening doors and following them through the pre-op hallway. Once in the clinic, Nola cleaned the wound and prepared for surgery.

Chuck faded in and out. The overhead lamps made his face glow. She injected a sedative. There was a period where he floated and dreamed among the stars. The Milky Way was within grasp, the way he'd seen it the night before at the cemetery. He floated in space, kissing stars and ricocheting off planets, a transitive nightfall of diamonds, before landing safely on the medical bed.

It was the next day or the day after when Phobos' wristwatch had finally died. Time had stopped out here in this peaceable kingdom. At night it was a whole other dimension. Owls hooted, cats growled, coyotes howled. The sky was so black that the stars, planets and the Milky Way truly did look like they could be touched and grabbed by human hands.

Daylight was bright as heaven, the clouds fluffy and cuddly. Birds chirped, turkeys strutted, cats climbed, tumbled, or laid in the shade.

"Your debt's been taken care of, boo." Nola said. She had her arm around Chuck who had one arm in a sling. "You see that bump in the dirt over there? That's where your debt is."

"It is? Wait. You buried money there?"

"Nah, booboo. Just what was sucking the life and air from everything and everybody. The man with no legs will no longer be a plague on to you."

"Boots?" Chucks mouth fell open.

"Yes, it is. *But*. Remember that favor I needed?"

"Yeah."

"I want his van out of here. You know anybody who can chop it?"

"We can get Flames to do it." Chuck said. "He could be here in a few hours. I'll call him."

"You wanna stick around here while you recover?"

Propped up on his cane, Chuck took a gander at the landscape. The fresh graves gave him a chill.

"I'd love to. But not too long. I have to go feed Princess, okay?"

"You're not going to Mexico with *them*, are you?"

"Nah."

"Stay as long as you need," Nola said, and her eyes softened.

"How about you?"

"Make sure you get that van out of here. I have some things I have to go burn." She went inside her home with nothing further to say to Phobos or The Professor.

"I'm not going with you guys," Chuck said.

“I heard,” said Phobos. “I was standing right here when you told her.”

“I think I need a day or two to get better. Then I’ll catch a bus back. Listen, her witchcraft is bullshit, but I like her.”

“Her witchcraft healed us.” The Professor said.

“Actually, it was her medical skills that saved you both.” Phobos said. “I’m taking the Caddy back to Roy. Then I’ll hop a Greyhound and see how far it takes me. Eventually, I’ll meet up with Freebird. See what that’s about. Go dig some graves down there. Eat some tacos.”

“Everything will be as promised,” The Professor said.

Everything he’d lectured them about Mexico in the last day: the people, the landscape, politics, corruption. Regional foods. Beaches, dialects, clothing. How to be an American there. How to have a billion-dollar bash on $5 a day.

“The established government is questionable,” he’d told them. *“The great empires fell and it’s all just leftovers now. White man’s fault, no doubt. Colonialism. Territorialism. Elitism. Etc.”*

Phobos envisaged the heat, tacos on the beach, playing guitar under a tree, silhouetted soccer players at sunset, Freebird among them. Pants optional.

They regrouped by the Great White.

“Oh shit.” Chuck suddenly panicked. “Aw fuck. I forgot to tell you. Don’t open the trunk just yet. Shit. Freebird stuffed *something* in there. Forgot to dump it when we got to Bardo.”

Phobos rubbed his forehead.

“Is it dead?” he said.

“Very,” said Chuck.

For the next hour they watched Phobos dig a grave behind the old mobile home and bury the man in the brown suit and green tie, with the face that had been eaten away.

"Sorry, buddy." Chuck said.

Phobos ignored him. When he finished, he rinsed off with the garden house and dried off at the car.

"This *shark* took good care of us," said Chuck. He patted the hood of the Cadillac and kissed it. "It's a fucking tank. Sorry about the bullet holes. And the smell."

"I'll get Harold to fix the damage before I leave for Mexico." Phobos said.

"Gentlemen," The Professor said. He was hugging his briefcase. "What's our status?"

"I'm staying, he's going," Chuck said.

"Very well, Mr. Phobos. If you'd kindly drive me back to Atlanta, I will gladly pay you for gas. Also, I'd like to ride along with you to the Border. See what kind of distribution deal I can manage once I'm down there. Maybe teach a village how to make the most of their resources."

"White man speaks with forked tongue." Phobos said. "But do whatever you want, man."

"Perhaps I'll build my own laboratory there. Recreate my formula for LSD99 and print it on their currency."

"Just put it in their water," said Chuck. "Psychedelisize *Mejico*."

"I'm going to find Freebird," Phobos said. "Once I do, you're on your own, Professor."

Everyone shook hands, hugged.

"I feel good," Chuck said. "The good guys won."

"Is that what happened?" Phobos said. He straightened his messy shirt, tightened his headband, and adjusted his glasses. "Maybe this round. We'll always be losers."

"Gentlemen," The Professor said. "You're lone wolves among dead dogs. You're just waiting your turn."

CPSIA information can be obtained
at www.ICGtesting.com
Printed in the USA
BVHW030415270820
587448BV00002B/517

9 781945 181894